KAIZEN DISRUPTION

SMALL STEPS, GIANT LEAPS IN BUSINESS AND TECHNOLOGY

HIMANSHU JAIN

PRABHAT
PRAKASHAN

No part of this publication can be reproduced, stored in a retrieval system or transmitted in any form or by any means, electronic, mechanical, photocopying, recording or otherwise, without the prior permission of the author and the publisher.

Published by
PRABHAT PRAKASHAN PVT. LTD.
4/19 Asaf Ali Road,
New Delhi-110 002 (INDIA)
e-mail: prabhatbooks@gmail.com

ISBN 978-93-5562-961-6
KAIZEN DISRUPTION: SMALL STEPS, GIANT LEAPS IN BUSINESS AND TECHNOLOGY
by Himanshu Jain

© Reserved

Edition
First, 2024

Price
₹ 300.00 (Rupees Three Hundred only)

Printed at
Sita Fine Arts Pvt. Ltd., Delhi

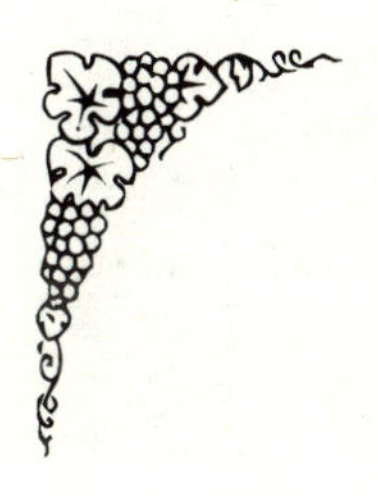

To

my parents

for their unwavering support

and

for motivating me

to write this book.

Author's Note

The concept of Kaizen has had a profound impact on me, both personally and professionally. As someone deeply fascinated by philosophies of continuous improvement, I was immediately drawn to Kaizen's emphasis on making small, incremental changes to achieve long-lasting progress.

What initially struck me about Kaizen was its counterintuitive nature compared to our cultural tendency to seek revolutionary, large-scale change. The more I studied Kaizen's origins in Japanese manufacturing and its principles of gradual refinement, the more I became convinced of its wisdom and effectiveness.

In researching and writing this piece, I was particularly inspired by Kaizen's core idea that sustainable transformation happens not through radical disruption, but by systematically implementing minor enhancements over time. This sidesteps the mental resistance we often encounter with 'big bang' change initiatives.

My goal is to shed light on Kaizen's powerful simplicity. While it arose in a manufacturing context, I believe its teachings have universal applicability—whether you're an individual striving for self-improvement, a leader aiming to enhance your organisation, or simply someone seeking a mindset of ongoing optimisation in your daily life.

I hope this exploration of Kaizen's origins, principles and far-reaching impacts will inspire you to embrace its philosophy of continual refinement. Small, steady steps can pave the way for remarkable progress when implemented with patience and discipline. I sincerely wish this work provides a fresh perspective and perhaps even a life-changing paradigm shift. Prepare to rethink your approach to growth and change.

Acknowledgements

I am profoundly grateful to my parents and my brother for their unwavering support and encouragement throughout the writing process. Their belief in my capabilities and their consistent motivation has served as the cornerstone of my endeavour. Their encouragement, both in my professional pursuits as a software engineer and in my literary endeavours, has significantly contributed to the development of this book. Their invaluable insights and unwavering support have empowered me to disseminate my ideas to a wider audience.

I extend my heartfelt thanks to all who have played a pivotal role in this journey.

Contents

Author's Note 5

Acknowledgements 7

1. Introduction 11
2. What is Kaizen? 13
3. Application of Kaizen 22
4. The Great Pillars of Kaizen 29
5. Elimination of Waste 35
6. Kaizen and Innovation 42
7. Kaizen to Create Lasting Excellence 51
8. QCD and Kaizen Goals 62
9. Rewards and Recognition Functions of Kaizen 68
10. TMQ and Kaizen 75
11. Group Activities 81
12. Measurement of Kaizen Effect 89

13.	How Kaizen Affects Nutritional Habits?	96
14	Use Kaizen to Improve Sleep	102
15	Studying and Kaizen	111
16	The PDCA Cycle	121
17	Conquering Fear and Stress	126
18	Don't Be Hard on Yourself	135

1

Introduction

Kaizen is a Japanese term that means 'improvement' and refers to both significant and minor enhancements as well as continuous or singular progress. It is a Japanese business philosophy that focuses on continuous improvement in processes, practices and products. The term 'Kaizen' is composed of the Japanese words 'kai' (change) and 'zen' (good), and it encapsulates the idea of making small, gradual and ongoing enhancements to enhance efficiency, quality and overall performance. In certain contexts, such as martial arts like Kungfu, it conveys the notion of gradual but meticulous advancement. The business sector worldwide has notably achieved substantial progress through the application of Kaizen principles.

Business culture often values the idea of sudden and revolutionary change. However, attempts at turnaround often falter because radical shifts trigger our brain's fear response, hindering clear and creative thinking. A more effective approach to change starts with small, incremental steps of Kaizen. These gradual actions bypass our mental alarm system, allowing creativity and intellectual processes to flow freely. Consequently, the change achieved is long-lasting and impactful. Leaders frequently face the challenge of making significant improvements to their organisations, be it cost reduction, product innovation, error minimisation, or service enhancement. While it may seem tempting to push through obstacles with sheer determination, lasting improvements can be achieved through the methodical application of Kaizen principles.

Kaizen originally emerged in Japan, within the manufacturing sector, as a set of techniques and tools designed to enhance productivity and quality. Over time, it has gained global recognition. While there are various perspectives regarding the scope and comprehension of Kaizen, we will focus on its core values. These values encourage a shared attitude among members of organisations who are striving for sustained advancements in productivity and quality. It is important to note that Kaizen isn't merely a management methodology confined within organisational frameworks. Instead, it embodies an adaptable and flexible approach that practitioners can readily embrace.

❑

2

What is Kaizen?

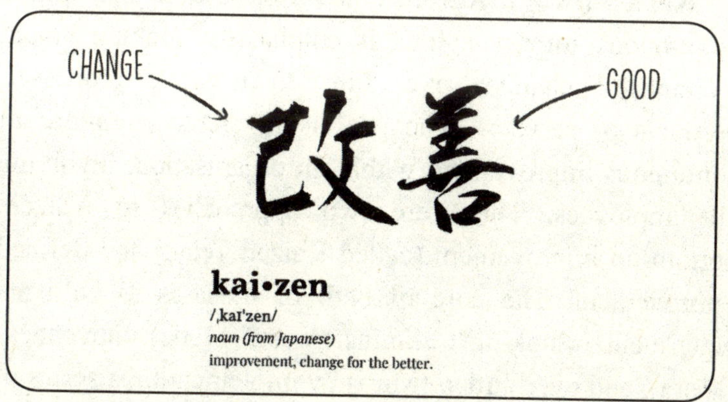

The Kaizen approach pertains to a specific process improvement that is achieved within a set timeframe to meet a goal or objective, unlike continuous improvement, which is comparatively more spontaneous than this. It requires thoughtful planning rather than just suggestions made by the project lead, which is the Teian (suggestion) approach. It addresses specific challenges instead of overall improvement to bring about a step change in efficiency, quality or performance. However, all events must align with broader operational goals and processes to have a sustained impact. Kaizen focuses on continuous improvement through small, incremental changes, Kaikaku involves radical transformations to achieve breakthrough results, Kakushin entails revolutionary innovation and new ways of thinking, and Liji refers to adherence to established customs or traditions without significant change.

Kaizen (改善): Kaizen is a Japanese term that means 'continuous improvement'. It emphasises making small, incremental changes over time to improve processes, products or services. The goal is to create a culture of continuous improvement within an organisation, involving all employees. There are two approaches to Kaizen: bottom-up improvement (called Kaizen Teian) and defined improvement. The core of both of those is to cultivate betterment by looking to eliminate waste (Muda), unevenness (Mura), and overburden (Muri) by implementing a series of continuous, incremental minor improvement steps.

Kaikaku (改革): Kaikaku, also known as 'radical change' or 'breakthrough improvement', is a more drastic approach compared to Kaizen. Kaizen focuses on gradual improvements, while Kaikaku involves implementing significant and transformative changes to processes or systems. It often requires rethinking existing methods and may even involve restructuring or redesigning entire processes to achieve breakthrough results. Unlike Kaizen,

Kaikaku is about radical change. It may demand the organisation moves to an entirely new process, such as moving from manual to automated production or embarking on a digital transformation that drives workplace collaboration. Hiroyuki Hirano developed the *5S system that offers the Ten Commandments of Kaikaku.*

Kakushin (革新): If Kaikaku is revolutionary, Kakushin is game-changing. Kakushin is a term that refers to 'innovation' or 'revolutionary change'. It involves introducing new ideas, technologies or approaches to fundamentally transform an organisation or industry. Kakushin requires challenging existing norms and paradigms to bring about radical shifts in thinking and practices. Unlike Kaizen and Kaikaku, which focus on improving existing processes, Kakushin involves creating entirely new ways of operating. It's about introducing the big breakthrough that changes everything. While Kaikaku may involve making a major change in how things are done, Kakushin may be about changing what is done. For instance, if Kaikaku is about moving from manual to automated production, Kakushin would be the switch to 3D printing those materials, demanding new skills from the workforce.

Liji (維持): Liji is a Chinese term that means sustainability. It refers to 'established customs' or 'rituals'. In the context of business or management, it refers to following established practices or traditions, without emphasising change or improvement. Unlike the other terms mentioned, Liji maintains stability and continuity by following established norms and customs. This is considered the most vital element and a *pre-requisite for Kaizen* as said by Taiichi Ohno himself: "Without standards, there can be no Kaizen."

The state of Liji is about being able to sustain any improvement that has been accomplished as a foundation for the next improvement push. If an organisation is resistant to change and always falls back to its original state, then it cannot sustain any change. Hence, any effort put into driving Kaizen would be for naught.

Kaizen is a philosophy of continuous improvement that is central to the Toyota Production System (TPS). Three key terms that are often discussed in Kaizen are: Muda, (無駄), Muri (無理), and Mura (斑). Let us take a closer look at them.

1. **Muda:** Muda translates to 'waste' in Japanese. In the context of Kaizen, Muda refers to any activity that consumes resources (time, money, materials) without adding value to the product or service from the customer's perspective. Seven types of Muda are commonly identified in Lean thinking:

   - *Overproduction:* Producing more than what is needed.
   - *Waiting:* Idle time between processes or tasks.
   - *Transportation:* Unnecessary movement of materials or products.
   - *Overprocessing:* Doing more work than necessary.
   - *Inventory:* Excess inventory that ties up resources.

- *Motion:* Unnecessary movement of people.
- *Defects:* Rework or scrap due to errors.

Understanding and eliminating Muda is key to improving efficiency and productivity in any process.

2. **Muri:** Muri means 'overburden' or 'overexertion'. It refers to the strain or stress placed on people, equipment or processes due to excessive or unreasonable demands. Muri often leads to inefficiencies, errors and workplace injuries. In Kaizen, eliminating sources of Muri is crucial for creating a smoother and more sustainable workflow.

3. **Mura:** Mura translates to 'unevenness' or 'variation'. It refers to irregularities or inconsistencies in the workflow, such as fluctuations in demand, uneven workloads, or inconsistent processes. Mura can cause inefficiencies, overburden (Muri), and waste (Muda). Kaizen aims to reduce Mura by standardising processes, levelling workloads, and creating a more balanced workflow.

Identifying and addressing Muda, Muri and Mura can help organisations to improve efficiency, quality and customer satisfaction while reducing costs and lead times. These concepts are fundamental to the continuous improvement philosophy of Kaizen and are applied across various industries to achieve operational excellence.

How did Kaizen Emerge?

Kaizen, a methodology that involves incremental steps for continuous improvement, was first systematically applied in Depression-era America. With the onset of the Second World War, the American leaders recognised the Allies' critical need for military equipment shipments and the possibility of American soldiers being deployed overseas. This necessitated the production of tanks, weapons and supplies on a large scale. However, American manufacturers faced the challenge of rapidly increasing both the quality and quantity of their equipment production. Furthermore, many skilled factory supervisors were enlisted in the American armed forces, leaving a shortage of experienced personnel in the manufacturing sector.

To address the pressing time and personnel limitations, the US Government introduced management courses known as Training Within Industries (TWI), that were made available to corporations nationwide. These courses laid the early roots of what would later be recognised as Kaizen. Unlike advocating for radical or revolutionary changes to meet demands, TWI emphasised the concept of 'continuous improvement'. The course materials encouraged supervisors to focus on identifying numerous small enhancements rather than attempting major overhauls such as department layout redesigns or large-scale equipment installations, given the urgency of the situation. The emphasis was on improving existing processes and tasks with the available resources, rather than pursuing extensive and time-consuming transformations.

The US faced intense time pressure to produce weapons and equipment faster than ever before. Elitism and snobbery became indulgences, no longer affordable. From the lowest ranks to those in the most influential positions, everyone was urged to seek out small methods to enhance product quality and production efficiency. This approach led to placement of suggestion boxes on factory floors, giving line workers a chance to propose productivity improvements, and requiring executives to consider each suggestion with utmost respect. This egalitarian approach fostered a culture where contributions from all levels of the organisation were valued and considered integral to achieving success.

Though this may have appeared inadequate at first, the accumulation of many small improvements led to a significant increase in the country's manufacturing capacity. The combination of improved quality in American equipment and increased speed of production emerged as two pivotal factors contributing to the Allied victory. Despite initial scepticism, the effectiveness of the incremental approach became evident as it helped the US to meet the demands of wartime production.

During the post-war era in Japan, General Douglas MacArthur's occupation forces introduced the philosophy of gradual improvement through small steps as part of the reconstruction efforts. Despite Japan's later corporate dominance in the late 20th century, many of its businesses at that time were poorly managed, with lax practices and low employee morale. General MacArthur recognised the need to enhance Japanese efficiency and elevate business standards. A thriving Japanese economy was essential as it could serve as a bulwark against potential threats from North Korea and ensure steady supplies for his troops. To achieve this, MacArthur enlisted the expertise of TWI specialists from the US Government, who emphasised the significance of incremental, daily changes. Additionally, the US Air Force provided management and supervision classes for Japanese businesses near its local bases, further reinforcing the importance of improved practices and efficiency.

The US Air Force introduced the Management Training Programme (MTP) which had striking similarities with the principles developed by Dr Deming (a statistician and economist) and his colleagues during the war. Thousands of Japanese business managers participated in this programme, reflecting a widespread commitment to adopting modern management practices and promoting a culture of continuous improvement.

The Japanese were surprisingly open to the idea of viewing employees as a source of creativity and improvement, despite it being unfamiliar territory for both Japanese and American business cultures. Their industrial infrastructure was devastated after the war, leaving them with limited means for reorganisation. Moreover, the defeat of Japan by the superior equipment and technology of the

US during the war compelled Japanese business leaders to pay close attention to the lessons on manufacturing imparted by the Americans.

The graduates of these programmes were enthusiastic about this approach and embraced it. As they transitioned into roles within civilian industries, they eagerly propagated the ethos of incremental improvement. These entrepreneurs, managers and executives became evangelists for the philosophy of small steps, contributing to its widespread adoption across various sectors of Japanese industry.

After the Second World War, Dr Deming's strategies for improving the manufacturing process were ignored in the US once production returned to normal. However, in Japan, his concepts were already taking root in the emerging business culture. In the late 1950s, the Japanese Union of Scientists and Engineers (JUSE) sought Dr Deming's expertise, recognising his role as a champion of quality control during the war. They invited him to further consult on enhancing their country's economic efficiency and output.

Japanese businesses have a reputation for achieving unprecedented levels of productivity thanks to their foundation of incremental improvements. These small steps proved so effective that the Japanese coined a term for them: 'Kaizen'. The term 'Kaizen' was coined and popularised by Masaaki Imai, a Japanese business consultant and founder of the Kaizen Institute.

❑

3

Applications of Kaizen

Kaizen is a term that is synonymous with continuous improvement and it involves engaging every individual in an organisation, from top executives to middle and lower-level managers. The essence of Kaizen is deeply ingrained in the mindset of every worker and manager. Often, they may not be consciously aware that they're thinking in the Kaizen manner. It becomes a natural approach driven by a focus on meeting customer needs and enhancing organisational performance.

Kaizen originally emerged in Japan's manufacturing industry, as a set of techniques and tools aimed at improving productivity and quality. Its importance has been recognised globally. While interpretations of Kaizen may differ, its core values focus on instilling a shared attitude among organisation members who are committed to consistently achieving advanced levels of productivity and quality. Importantly,

Kaizen isn't limited to organisational management methods; it embodies adaptability and flexibility, readily adjusting to various contexts and requirements.

Characteristics

- ***Participatory:*** Kaizen is highly effective because of its participatory approach. It unleashes the creativity and expertise of the entire organisation, from the C-suite to the shop floor, to achieve continuous, sustainable enhancements in quality, efficiency and overall business performance. Kaizen promotes participation across all levels of the organisational hierarchy.

  The Kaizen approach emphasises active participation and input from employees at every level, from top management to frontline workers. This participatory nature is crucial to the success of Kaizen initiatives. At the top, Kaizen requires strong leadership and commitment from senior executives who must foster a culture that embraces continuous improvement and empowers employees to identify and implement changes. They serve as role models and champion the Kaizen mindset throughout the organisation. Middle managers play a vital coordinating role, ensuring Kaizen activities are properly supported, resourced and aligned with broader organisational goals. They facilitate the flow of ideas and feedback between frontline staff and senior leadership. Kaizen places a significant emphasis on drawing insights and suggestions from frontline workers since they are closest to the actual processes and operations. They often have the best understanding of where improvements can be made. Kaizen encourages them to share their ideas, no matter their position in the hierarchy. By tapping into the collective intelligence of the entire workforce, Kaizen harnesses the power of participatory problem-solving. This bottom-up approach helps identify and resolve issues quickly while cultivating employee ownership and engagement in the improvement process.

- ***Continuous:*** The Kaizen philosophy is founded on the belief that continuous, small-scale improvements, when accumulated over time, can lead to transformative results. Rather than pursuing dramatic, one-time overhauls, Kaizen encourages a methodical, scientific approach to problem-solving and process enhancement. The core of this continuous improvement mindset is the realisation that making many small adjustments on a daily basis can have a profound long-term impact. Kaizen activities focus on identifying and addressing tiny inefficiencies, bottlenecks, or sources of waste through observation and analysis of relevant data.

This approach is based on a scientific method that involves collecting and analysing relevant metrics and statistics. Kaizen practitioners closely monitor key performance indicators, quality measures, and other data points to identify areas for improvement. They then formulate hypotheses, test potential solutions, and meticulously monitor the outcomes.

By anchoring Kaizen in objective data and a rigorous, iterative problem-solving methodology, organisations can ensure that their continuous improvement efforts are based on facts rather than assumptions. This evidence-based approach helps substantiate the impact of even the tiniest changes, building confidence and momentum for further improvements.

Kaizen emphasises the importance of making continuous improvements a regular habit across the organisation. Employees are encouraged to continuously scan their work environments, proactively identify problems, and implement immediate, incremental fixes. This daily discipline of small-scale problem-solving is what ultimately leads to transformative, large-scale changes over time. By using a scientific, data-driven approach, Kaizen unlocks the power of gradual, compounding improvements to drive sustained organisational excellence.

- ***Economical:*** The economic aspect of Kaizen is a crucial dimension that goes beyond just financial considerations. It emphasises the value of human wisdom and ingenuity, which can be leveraged even in the face of limited resources. At its core, Kaizen is about maximising efficiency and optimising processes through creative problem-solving. Instead of solely focusing on increasing capital investments or expenditures, Kaizen encourages organisations to utilise the intellectual and experiential capital of their employees. The Kaizen approach recognises that an organisation's most valuable resource comprises the collective knowledge, skills, and problem-solving abilities of its workforce. By empowering frontline workers to identify and implement improvements, Kaizen taps into a wellspring of insights that can drive meaningful change, even in resource-constrained environments.

This economic approach of Kaizen is particularly relevant in developing economies or industries facing budgetary constraints. When financial resources are limited, Kaizen provides a cost-effective pathway to enhance productivity, improve quality and enhance competitiveness. It enables organisations to achieve more with less by promoting a culture of continuous improvement, creative thinking, and efficient utilisation of existing resources.

The economic nature of Kaizen means that it encourages improvements that do not require major financial investments including process streamlining, waste elimination, workplace organisation, or simple tool modifications. Rather than focusing solely on capital-intensive upgrades or expansions, Kaizen emphasises low-cost, high-impact changes that can be quickly implemented. It emphasises the power of human wisdom and ingenuity over financial resources. It enables organisations to become more resilient, adaptable, and economically sustainable, even in challenging circumstances. This economical approach has made Kaizen successful in diverse industries and regions around the world.

- ***Universal:*** The Kaizen philosophy is not restricted to any specific industry or business context. Its fundamental principles and practices can be effectively applied in manufacturing, service, healthcare, government, education and a wide range of other domains. This universal applicability of Kaizen is rooted in its focus on continuous improvement, waste elimination, and employee empowerment—principles that are universally relevant regardless of the nature of the organisation or the products/services it provides.

  Kaizen can be customised to meet the unique needs and constraints of any given organisation, regardless of its size or geographic location. Whether it's a large multinational corporation or a small local business, Kaizen can be adapted to drive meaningful enhancements in efficiency, quality and overall performance. In fact, the universal appeal of Kaizen has led to its global adoption, with organisations across developed and developing economies embracing its principles. From Japan, where it originated, to the United States, Europe and beyond, the Kaizen approach has proven effective in diverse cultural and economic contexts. This universality is a testament to the fundamental human-centric nature of Kaizen. By empowering employees at all levels to identify and resolve problems, Kaizen taps into the inherent problem-solving capabilities of the workforce, which are universally present regardless of the organisation's industry, size or location. The scientific, data-driven approach of Kaizen allows for it to be systematically applied and measured for results, making it a versatile improvement methodology. In essence, the universal applicability of Kaizen is a key reason for its enduring success and widespread adoption as a proven, effective approach to driving continuous improvement and organisational excellence in a range of industries and settings.

❑

4

The Great Pillars of Kaizen

The essence of Kaizen lies in the deep knowledge and confidence of the employees who carry out the tasks. By empowering these individuals to take ownership of the process, Kaizen instils a sense of responsibility that exceeds expectations. This collaborative team effort encourages innovation and facilitates change, involving employees at all levels. Kaizen breaks down organisational silos, allowing for more productive improvements across the entire system. It is not limited to manufacturing; Kaizen is everyone's business, as it's based on the fundamental principle that everyone is interested in improvement.

Kaizen is a process that aims to make the job of each individual easier by breaking down tasks, analysing their components, and making necessary improvements. This method is universal, as every employee contributes to the continuous improvement process. Masaaki Imai, the proponent of Kaizen, identified three pillars that are crucial for its success:

- **Visual management:** This involves ensuring that all employees have access to transparent and accessible information.
- **The role of supervisors:** Effective leadership and guidance from supervisors play an important role in Kaizen.
- **Creating a learning organisation:** Prioritising training and development helps to foster a culture of continuous improvement.

The success of Kaizen lies in the alignment and collaboration between management and employees, ensuring that everyone is invested in and contributing to the organisation's continuous improvement journey.

The 5S of Kaizen Activities

In the Kaizen philosophy, the workplace is referred to as the Gemba, which is the Japanese term for the place where actual value-adding work is done before products or services are passed on to the next stage. Managing the Gemba is a critical aspect of Kaizen, as it concentrates on the continuous improvement of the real work environment and processes. To facilitate effective Gemba management, Kaizen utilises the 5S methodology, which is derived from five Japanese words: Seiri (organisation), Seiton (orderliness), Seiso (cleanliness), Seiketsu (standardisation), and Shitsuke (discipline), In simpler terms, it involves sorting and straightening, sweeping and sanitising, and maintaining a tidy work environment.

- **Seiri:** Seiri is the Japanese term for sorting and it involves distinguishing necessary items from unnecessary ones. To make this process easy, the red tag system is used to label items that are deemed non-essential. It's important to involve everyone in the decision-making process to ascertain the necessity of these items before disposal. Red-tagged items should then be disposed of through sale to scrap dealers, donation, selling to employees, or disposal.
- **Seiton:** Seiton, also known as straightening, is a process of arranging essential items in a systematic way that ensures easy accessibility and visibility. Tools and other items should be clearly designated and stored in visible locations, often with outlines or pegs to indicate their proper place. Adhering to the principle of 'a place for everything, and everything in its place' helps maintain order and efficiency in the workspace.
- **Seiso:** Seiso, or cleanliness, entails thoroughly cleaning all remaining items to ensure they are free of dirt and grime. Consider painting or refreshing them to enhance their visual appeal and create a more aesthetically pleasing environment.
- **Seiketsu:** Seiketsu, also known as standardisation, involves creating and maintaining standardised

practices across the organisation. After improvements are made in a particular area through Kaizen initiatives, it's essential to share those improvements with others and provide them with the necessary training and resources to implement similar changes in their respective work areas. This results in consistency and efficiency throughout the company.

- **Shitsuke:** Shitsuke, the final step in the 5S methodology, focuses on maintaining standardisation and self-discipline. It involves establishing a regular cleaning schedule and utilising downtime to tidy and organise your work area. It helps to develop a habit of cleanliness and orderliness, which in turn contributes to a more efficient and productive work environment.

Benefits of 5S

The 5S methodology has become an essential tool for manufacturing organisations, as it helps elevate them to world-class status through improved workplace organisation and continuous improvement. By applying the 5S approach within the Gemba, Kaizen aims to create an organised, clean and efficient work environment that supports ongoing improvement and value creation. This holistic focus on managing the workplace is a key tenet of the Kaizen philosophy.

1. **Creating Clean, Pleasant and Safe Work Environments:** Creating clean, pleasant and safe work

environments is essential for boosting productivity and employee wellbeing. The 5S principles of sorting, straightening, shining, standardising, and sustaining help establish a work environment that is visually appealing, well-organised, and free of clutter and hazards. This enhances the overall physical work conditions, making the workplace more comfortable, safe and conducive to productivity.

2. **Revitalising the Workplace and Boosting Employee Motivation:** The 5S methodology involves employees in the implementation and maintenance process. This helps to cultivate a sense of ownership and pride in the work environment. This revitalisation of the workplace can have a powerful motivational effect, as employees feel valued and invested in their surroundings. Higher levels of employee motivation and morale contribute to improved engagement, job satisfaction, and overall performance.

3. **Minimising Waste Through Streamlined Tool Accessibility:** The 5S methodology comprises practices such as sorting and setting items in a specific order to ensure that frequently used tools and resources are readily accessible to operators. This streamlined accessibility reduces wasted time and effort spent searching for or retrieving necessary items, thereby simplifying the tasks and enhancing efficiency. By eliminating non-value-added activities, 5S helps minimise waste and optimise the overall workflow.

4. **Reducing Physical Strain and Freeing Up Workspace:** The principles of 5S encompass ergonomic considerations that include rearranging workstations and organising supplies. This helps minimise physical strain and fatigue for employees. The decluttering and optimisation of the work area also free up valuable workspace, allowing for better movement and collaboration among team members. These improvements in the physical work environment contribute to better employee health, comfort and productivity.

5. **Fostering a Sense of Belonging and Camaraderie:** The shared responsibility and commitment to maintaining the 5S principles create a sense of collective ownership and belonging among employees. Collaborating on 5S initiatives and taking pride in a well-organised, clean work environment helps foster stronger team dynamics and a greater sense of camaraderie. This improved team spirit and cohesion can further enhance communication, problem-solving, and overall organisational effectiveness.

The 5S methodology, as part of the Kaizen framework, aims to create a work environment that supports continuous improvement and overall organisational excellence by addressing key aspects such as efficiency, engagement and employee-centricity.

❑

5

Elimination of Waste

In Japanese, the term 'Muda' refers to waste. This waste refers to activities that do not add value to the workplace. Work is considered to be a series of activities that add value, ranging from the raw materials to the finished products. Below are some examples of waste in a company.

A. In manufacturing, waste can be in the form of overproduction, shipping defective parts, having excess inventory, transporting parts, and waiting for inspection.

B. In an office setting, waste can be found in activities such as routing documents, bureaucracy, and signature approvals, having a lot of papers and files, excess documentation, and passing on error-filled work.

The Seven (7) Deadly Wastes

Kaizen is a philosophy that aims to eliminate all these wastes. Seven (7) types of waste that are harmful and considered 'deadly'.

1. **Overproduction:** This occurs when there is machine failure, employee absenteeism, and rejection of products. Sometimes, companies try to produce more than what is necessary, bringing about tremendous waste. This leads to wasteful use of resources such as utilities, human resources and raw materials. Overproduction also causes an increase in the burden of interest, administrative and transportation costs, requires additional space to store excess inventory, etc.

2. **Motion:** Workers should avoid any type of motion that does not add value to production, as it is considered a waste. Activities such as lifting, walking, or carrying heavy objects that would require a great deal of effort should be avoided as it is risky and time-consuming. Rearranging the workplace to eliminate unnecessary movements can help improve efficiency.

3. **Defects:** Production interruptions, rejected products, and the need for rework are all examples of wasteful use of efforts and resources. These rejected products may require additional time to repair, increase the amount of time spent on inspection, require workers to be on standby at all times to stop the machines when necessary, and also increase paperwork.

4. **Waiting:** Idle operators result in waiting, which is a waste of time. Waiting can occur if an operator's work is put on hold either because of limited parts or downtime. Lead time in manufacturing starts when the company pays for the raw materials that are needed for the production of the item and ends when the company has received payment from the customers for the product. Lead time refers to the turnover of money. When there is a shorter lead time, it merely means that resources are utilised wisely, there is an excellent level of flexibility in meeting customer needs, and less is spent on operations. The elimination of waste is a very significant opportunity for Kaizen, and time waste is a type of waste in this category. When time is wasted, products, materials, documentation and information are dormant and add no value to the company.

5. **Inventory:** Inventory wastes refer to semi-finished products, final products, and part supplies that are kept in the inventory but do not add value to the company or the production process. Instead, they add to the cost of operations by taking up valuable space and requiring additional equipment and facilities such as forklifts, computerised conveyor systems, and storage units to store them. Whenever these products are kept for a long time, they may deteriorate in quality. When there is a change in the market value, customers desire a taste for new products, or if there is an introduction of new products, the product becomes obsolete. Additionally,

the storage units require additional administration and manpower to operate and are also prone to damage through disaster or fire. To address this issue, the introduction and initialisation of the Just-In-Time production system is recommended.

6. **Processing:** There are several ways in which waste can occur during processing. For example, when processes are not synchronised, it can lead to inefficiencies. This can be resolved by redesigning assembly lines to reduce the utilisation of input while producing the same number of outputs. Inputs include materials, utilities and resources, while outputs are the products required by the customers, services to be provided, added value, and yield. Redesigning the assembly line can involve reducing the number of workers to minimise errors and quality problems.

   This does not necessarily mean having to dismiss employees. They can be assigned to other sections for production. By increasing productivity, the cost of production will be reduced. In the manufacturing industry, long production lines require more workers, leading to more work-in-process and longer lead time, which can increase the possibility of errors and quality problems. Therefore, reducing the number of workers on the line can help improve the production process.

7. **Transportation:** Transportation is an essential part of the manufacturing industry, involving the use of forklifts,

trucks, and conveyors. However, the movements of materials do not add value to the production of the items and there is always a risk of damage in transportation. To minimise waste, any process that seems distant from the mainline should be integrated into the mainline. Thus, reducing waste is a quick way for a company to improve its workplace operations.

Standardisation

In order to bring about changes in an industry, certain standards are set by the management of the organisation. Once they are in place, what would be left is to acquire flowers. Employees will review the established standards, and either correct any deviations within the organisation or advise the management to improve or change the standards accordingly.

The 5 Ms

To improve and maintain the improvement of the workflow of employees, top managers use management tools otherwise known as the 5 Ms. By keeping an eye on the 5 Ms, the top managers of the company can identify what is working and what is not in a process. The 5 Ms are as follows:

1. **Manpower:** Managers must have a good understanding of their employees. This helps them to assess if they are completing their assigned tasks correctly, identify any problems related to work, determine each employee's

skills, track absenteeism and the reasons behind them, and monitor employee morale. Having the right employees is crucial for running the business efficiently.

2. **Machines:** Apart from the employees, it is crucial for the top managers to have a comprehensive knowledge of every machine and tool in their respective departments. The managers should conduct regular checks to ensure that the machines are being properly maintained and are in excellent working order. Additionally, they must ensure that the items produced meet the highest quality standards and identify any defects in the machine.

3. **Materials:** In Kaizen, it is crucial to maintain a smooth flow of materials. Only the necessary materials should be present in a particular work. Any excess materials should be stored in a different location. Every workstation should have a predetermined level for each process, which should be strictly adhered to.

4. **Methods:** The workplace should adopt a standardised method in order to ensure that tasks are done correctly. This helps managers to identify if the tasks assigned to the different employees are correctly done or not. To ensure adherence to the standardised method, post diagrams and worksheets that outline quality control and sequence control for each process of the department or entire enterprise.

5. **Measurements:** In order to determine if a process is running as it should or if any improvements are

being made, production schedules and targets should be displayed prominently for all employees to see. It is also important to clearly mark gauges to show the operating ranges of the equipment. Once these tools are integrated into the culture of the enterprise, they can aid in ensuring that Kaizen creates long-lasting results in terms of productivity, safety, team morale, and profits of the organisation.

❑

Kaizen and Innovation

How can we define innovation? How do Kaizen and innovation connect? Innovation can be defined as the process of introducing something new and novel—that creates value and impacts the market or industry meaningfully. It often involves a paradigm shift or a significant departure from existing approaches. Innovation involves big, bold changes that have the potential to create competitive advantages and drive step-change improvements. It requires an entrepreneurial mindset, risk-taking, and a willingness to challenge the status quo. Successful organisations understand the value of both paradigm-shifting innovations and ongoing Kaizen efforts. They create environments that encourage big ideas while empowering employees to continuously enhance existing operations. This combination is a potent strategy for sustainable competitive advantage. Both Kaizen and innovation involve challenging assumptions, fostering creativity, learning through experimentation, and maintaining an unwavering commitment to creating value for customers and the organisation.

Below are the four main types of innovation:

- **Process Innovation:** This refers to significant improvements to production or delivery methods. It includes changes to equipment, software, skills and techniques utilised.
- **Organisational Innovation:** This is the implementation of new organisational methods for improving workplace organisation, external relations, or business practices.
- **Marketing Innovation:** This involves substantial changes to product design, packaging, promotion, pricing, placement, or advertising approaches.
- **Product Innovation:** This involves introducing goods or services that have been significantly improved, such as enhancements to materials, components, software, technical specifications, or functional characteristics.

This taxonomy highlights that innovation can occur across the entire value chain. It can occur in the way things are made (processes), how the organisation operates (structures), how offerings are marketed (promotions), and what products/services are brought to the market (goods/services). Managing and driving innovation effectively requires a multipronged approach that considers all these areas. Focusing solely on product innovation while ignoring processes, organisation, and go-to-market strategies, could limit the ability to maximise the impact of new offerings. By taking a holistic view of innovation opportunities across processes, organisation, marketing, and products/services, companies can better identify ways to create sustainable competitive advantages. Innovations can be categorised based on the degree or magnitude of change involved. There are two types of innovation in this dimension.

a. **Incremental Innovation:** Incremental innovation involves making significant upgrades, enhancements, or improvements to an existing product, service, process, method, or organisational approach. Incremental innovations build upon and refine current offerings or operations rather than completely reinventing them. Examples of incremental innovations include adding new product features, process optimisations, service additions, etc.

b. **Radical or Disruptive Innovation:** Radical innovations are game-changing breakthroughs that have a profound impact on markets and industries. These are innovations that disrupt the status quo by introducing entirely new paradigms, technologies, or business models. Radical innovations can redefine economic activities, reshape customer expectations, and render existing approaches obsolete. Examples of radical innovations include the introduction of the internet, smartphones, ride-sharing services, etc.

Incremental innovations provide evolutionary improvements and add value to the existing products or services. They allow companies to steadily increase value, remain competitive, and maximise profits from current capabilities. Radical innovations, on the other hand, are revolutionary and transformative in nature. They create new markets, drive exponential growth opportunities, and establish sustainable competitive advantages. Both types of innovations are necessary for a business to succeed.

Effective innovators are capable of managing an ambidextrous portfolio that balances incremental initiatives for the short-term, while also pursuing more radical, longer-term prospects. This multipronged innovation strategy can fuel an organisation's long-term viability and success. Incremental innovation is more common and dominant in business, while disruptive or radical innovation occurs less frequently but can have a transformative impact.

Incremental innovations build the foundation for breakthroughs and disruptive innovations. They are the small, incremental steps that advance technologies, processes, and business models until a tipping point is reached, allowing for a major leap forward. Incremental innovations can also entrench incumbents. Established companies tend to focus on incremental innovations to their core products/services, which makes them better at the status quo but also creates inertia that makes it difficult to pursue disruptive paths.

Disruptive innovations can arise from incremental efforts. The innovation process usually involves numerous incremental refinements and enhancements. In some cases, the cumulative effect of many incremental changes can enable or catalyse a disruptive shift. Disruptive innovations frequently have their roots in incremental innovation. Disruption paves the way for new waves of incremental innovation. Once a disruptive, game-changing innovation occurs, it unlocks new opportunities for continuous incremental innovation on that new platform, technology, or business model.

In many ways, incremental and disruptive innovation are complementary and interlinked. Although disruptive breakthroughs are rare, they have a higher impact. Prudent innovators cultivate an ambidextrous approach. This involves continuously pursuing incremental improvements while also exploring more transformative opportunities that could emerge from their incremental efforts.

Masaaki Imai's book *Gemba Kaizen* on the relationship between innovation and Kaizen

In Masaaki Imai's book *Gemba Kaizen – A Commonsense Approach to Continuous Improvement Strategy*, he highlights the relationship between Kaizen and innovation, presenting them as contrasting concepts. Innovation is usually attention-grabbing and dramatic, often resulting in major technological breakthroughs. On the other hand, Kaizen is depicted as subtle and incremental and involves a series of small improvements while not individually significant, collectively lead to transformative outcomes. Kaizen helps develop workers' skills and capacity, encouraging them to use statistical data to address real problems and maintain a continuous improvement mindset. Ultimately, Kaizen enhances the organisation's capabilities, enabling it to take appropriate actions, experiment with new ideas and solutions, and embrace innovative technologies to achieve meaningful outcomes.

So while Imai contrasted the magnitude of change between innovation and Kaizen initially, he also underscored how an organisational culture of Kaizen provides the foundation and skills required for more disruptive innovations to take hold successfully.

The key takeaway is that innovation and Kaizen are not mutually exclusive concepts but rather complement each other. Kaizen strengthens the capacity for innovation, while innovations create new opportunities for further Kaizen efforts.

Kaizen is a crucial factor that enables and supports successful innovation within an organisation. Following are some key ways Kaizen supports and feeds into the innovation process:

1. **Quality enhancement:** As you noted, Kaizen's relentless focus on improving quality lays the groundwork for innovations to build upon. Innovations are more likely to succeed when the baseline processes and quality standards are rigorously optimised through Kaizen.

2. **Human capital development:** Kaizen engages workers at all levels in problem-solving, skill-building, and adopting a mindset of continuous betterment. This develops the human capabilities critical for innovation.
3. **Process optimisation:** Kaizen's drive to incrementally enhance business processes, workflows, and operational efficiencies streamlines systems, reduces waste and frees up resources that can be channelled into innovation initiatives.
4. **Cultural foundation:** The discipline, data-driven approach, and emphasis on customer value instilled by Kaizen cultivate an organisational culture receptive to change and new ideas—fertile ground for innovations to grow.
5. **Rapid iteration:** The iterative PDCA (plan-do-cheque-act) cycles core to Kaizen create a mechanism for quickly piloting, refining, and implementing innovations through rapid experimentation loops.

So in many ways, Kaizen acts as both an input helping to create an innovation-conducive environment, while also facilitating the downstream implementation and optimisation of innovative ideas as an ongoing process.

You can make an astute observation that Kaizen is paramount to ultimately achieving innovative outputs across product quality, process efficiency, and management practices. A robust Kaizen programme provides the enabling infrastructure for an organisation to successfully innovate sustainably.

While quality is paramount, cost-effectiveness is an equally crucial factor that determines an organisation's success. Cost-effectiveness encompasses the overall expenditure incurred throughout the entire lifecycle of a product or service, spanning design, production, sales, and after-sales support. It is important to note that cost reduction is not merely about indiscriminate cost-cutting measures. Instead, it is a nuanced exercise in cost management.

Dedicated cost management teams are tasked with overseeing the development, manufacture and sale of high-quality products or services while simultaneously minimising costs. How a product is designed, produced and brought to market can significantly influence the degree of resource waste, making it a critical consideration. The ultimate objective is to strike a delicate balance between improving quality and reducing costs, as this synergy is vital for organisational survival and growth.

Cost management encompasses a wide spectrum of activities, ranging from overall cost reduction in the workplace by eliminating waste to developing strategies to maximise the margin between revenue and expenditure. The elimination of waste, a cornerstone of cost reduction, can be achieved through the implementation of various waste elimination methods discussed earlier.

However, it is crucial to recognise that indiscriminate cost-cutting measures, such as restructuring, pressuring suppliers, or laying off employees, can disrupt the quality process and potentially lead to a deterioration in quality standards. Therefore, cost management must be a holistic endeavour that encompasses activities such as standardisation, policy deployment, education, and training.

In the context of training, contemporary organisations often place excessive emphasis on imparting knowledge alone. In contrast, the Kaizen philosophy places great importance on the improvement of fundamental organisational values, which are cultivated through group learning environments. These values encompass self-discipline, common sense, economy and order, all of which are essential for fostering a culture of continuous improvement.

In essence, the passage highlights the importance of balancing quality and cost-effectiveness, the distinction between cost reduction and cost management, the role of dedicated teams in overseeing this balance, the potential consequences of indiscriminate cost-cutting measures, and the significance of fostering fundamental organisational values through group learning in the Kaizen approach.

❑

7

Kaizen to Create Lasting Excellence

Embracing the principles of Kaizen can significantly contribute to accomplishing your management goals. Kaizen advocates for continuous improvement through incremental steps. By adopting a Kaizen mindset, managers can cultivate a culture of constant improvement within their teams. Instead of waiting for major overhauls or radical changes, employees are encouraged to seek small improvements in their daily work processes. This approach fosters a sense of ownership and empowerment among team members, as they are actively involved in identifying areas for enhancement and implementing changes.

By breaking down objectives into smaller goals, Kaizen prevents employees from feeling overwhelmed by the enormity of their objectives and keeps the momentum going towards achieving them.

Kaizen promotes a mindset of experimentation and learning. Instead of fearing failure, employees are encouraged to try new approaches and learn from their mistakes. This not only facilitates innovation and creativity but also fosters a culture of continuous learning and development within the organisation. By embracing the principles of Kaizen, managers can create a dynamic and adaptive work environment where continuous improvement is not only encouraged but ingrained into the organisational culture, ultimately leading to greater efficiency, productivity, and success in achieving management goals.

Morale Boost

Boosting employee morale can be achieved through implementing strategies that demonstrate appreciation for employee contributions, fostering a positive work environment, and addressing underlying issues that may be dampening morale. For instance, one effective approach is to actively acknowledge and reward employees for their hard work and dedication. This can be achieved through gestures such as public recognition, bonuses, or other forms of incentives that show appreciation for their efforts.

It is important to address and resolve interpersonal conflicts or difficulties within the workplace as it can help alleviate tension and improve overall morale. Sometimes, removing or reassigning individuals who are causing disruptions or conflicts can contribute to a more harmonious work environment. This, in turn, allows employees to focus on their tasks without undue stress or distractions.

Encouraging employees to participate in problem-solving and decision-making processes can also boost morale by empowering them and fostering a sense of ownership and engagement in their work. By soliciting their input and involving them in finding solutions to challenges, employees feel valued and respected, ultimately leading to heightened morale and motivation levels.

Consider a scenario where the management identifies a decline in employee morale. In response, they may opt to invest in hiring consultants specialised in employee satisfaction, even if it means paying higher fees than usual. These consultants may devise strategies such as implementing regular breaks for employees, which can contribute to improving morale. Recognising the importance of compensating employees fairly for their work, management may also prioritise initiatives that demonstrate appreciation for their efforts, such as offering competitive salaries and benefits packages.

Furthermore, small gestures of gratitude, such as expressing thanks or offering tokens of appreciation, can have a significant impact on morale. Employees cherish feeling recognised and valued for their contributions, and simple acts of appreciation can go a long way in boosting morale and fostering a positive work culture. It's essential to address underlying factors that may be contributing to low morale, such as recent layoffs, wage freezes, or changes in incentive programmes. While employees may understand the challenges faced by the company, it's crucial to communicate openly and transparently about the reasons behind such decisions. Exploring alternative solutions that can mitigate the negative impact on morale is equally important.

Contain or Reduce Cost

The Kaizen methodology for cost control involves empowering employees to identify and eliminate processes that do not contribute to productivity or product/service quality. This approach prioritises the well-being of employees while striving for efficiency. In Kaizen-oriented companies, employees are encouraged to be vigilant for wasteful practices. Any process identified as unnecessary or inefficient is promptly removed, resulting in effective cost control.

While it may initially seem counterintuitive to entrust employees with cost control responsibilities, involving them in small steps towards saving company funds proves beneficial. However, the management must not solely burden employees with cost-reduction tasks, as this could create fear and hinder progress. Instead, management should guide employee approach to their daily tasks, enabling them to identify cost-saving opportunities. Building trust and fostering an open environment where employees feel comfortable suggesting ideas without fear of judgement or reprisal is crucial to successful implementation. Some of these include:

1. Taking the time to inquire about employees' weekend plans demonstrates a genuine interest in their well-

being beyond the workplace. This simple gesture fosters a sense of camaraderie and shows that you value their work-life balance, contributing to a positive and supportive work environment.

2. Acknowledging and greeting every employee you encounter within the workplace creates a welcoming atmosphere, promoting inclusivity and respect. By extending a friendly greeting, you reinforce the idea that each team member is valued and recognised, regardless of their role or position within the organisation.

3. Expressing appreciation when an employee submits a project underscores the importance of their contributions and efforts. Whether through verbal acknowledgement, a written note of thanks, or a small token of appreciation, recognising their hard work and dedication motivates employees to continue striving for excellence in their work.

4. Making an effort to remember the names of staff members throughout the organisation demonstrates attentiveness and respect for individual identities. Addressing colleagues by their names not only personalises interactions but also fosters a sense of belonging and mutual respect within the workplace community.

5. Leading by example sets a positive tone for the entire organisation and inspires others to emulate your behaviour. By demonstrating qualities such as integrity,

professionalism and dedication in your own actions and decisions, you establish clear expectations and norms for behaviour, guiding the team toward success through exemplary leadership.

The Kaizen approach to control costs helps employees identify and eliminate any process that does not enhance the productivity and quality of products and services. At the same time, Kaizen promotes the well-being of employees in any organisation.

In Kaizen-driven organisations, employees are encouraged to remain alert for wasted resources. When employees identify processes that do not add quality or increase value, they are removed. This ensures cost control is effective and efficient. While depending on employees for cost control may seem unproductive, encouraging them to take little steps towards saving company resources will prove invaluable.

The sole responsibility for cost reduction should not be assigned to employees. This would create fear in the employees and not allow change to happen. Instead, the management should shape the employees' approaches to their daily jobs in the enterprise, so that they can spot opportunities for savings.

Trust me, once the employees feel supported, they will be fully engaged in the process. As a leader, you should create an environment where employees can give suggestions without any fear. Thus, by effective communication, continuous improvement can happen in any organisation.

Steps to Controlling Cost

a. **Offer Little or No Rewards:** In Japan, employee suggestion plans have consistently yielded success, but in the United States, the opposite is often true. Research shows that in the United States, cash rewards are offered that are proportional to the money saved through employee suggestions. This motivates the employees to identify more cost-saving opportunities because of the greater rewards. In contrast, in Japan, there are either modest cash rewards or no rewards at all. Psychological studies have proven that human motivations are illuminating.

   Motivation is of two types: **extrinsic and intrinsic.**

   1. *Intrinsic motivation:* This type of motivation comes from within. They are the desire to contribute, engage in meaningful tasks, and also to take pride in their jobs. People with inner motivation seek challenges and are proud of what they do. They have an inner drive to do meaningful things.

   2. *Extrinsic motivation:* Extrinsic motivation comes with factors like monetary benefits and job titles. They can induce people to endure stressful work. The key to controlling costs is to make the rewards as small as possible. When there are cutbacks, one can still maintain a Kaizen outlook by ensuring the cuts are calm and thoughtful.

Thus, to control costs, do not rely on extrinsic motivation. Intrinsic motivation should be fostered by providing an environment that recognises employee efforts. While considering cost-control measures, adopting a Kaizen mindset can ensure that the reductions are maintained thoughtfully.

b. **Ask Small Questions:** Many managers try to ensure their employees provide continual improvement. However, they are aggressive in their tactics and this creates setbacks. This can lead to the employees feeling embarrassed or uncomfortable, hindering open communication.

For instance, asking the question, "What can be done to save the company millions of money?" can overwhelm employees, leading to a mental block. Instead, a gentle approach like "Can you suggest ways we can save money?" can encourage employees to respond without stress.

By inviting feedback from employees and valuing their opinions, managers can ensure efficiency in the workplace.

c. **Align Savings With the Mission of the Company:** To align savings with the mission of the company, the workplace should reflect our goals. By removing notice boards that fail to attract employees' attention, we are emphasising that the suggestions made are aligned with the company's mission.

Furthermore, by encouraging employees to make small suggestions, we reinforce the idea that small changes can contribute to the mission's success. Let us treasure these opportunities for positive change.

d. **Be Open to Suggestions:** Encourage employees to offer suggestions without fear of ridicule or reprimand. Adopt Kaizen principles by assigning employees to identify cost-saving opportunities. Maintain authority and be responsible for evaluating ideas. Set up procedures for managing suggestions. While filtering the suggestions given, take every one of them seriously. Differentiate stupidity from simplicity. Even the most basic suggestion may hold the key to genius. Do not forget to thank the employee whose suggestions brought about the change the company needed. Also, take the opportunity to enhance his skills through training. The Kaizen platform is thus a platform for continuous learning and employment.

Improve Quality of Products, Services and Personal Life

Enhancing our ability to locate mistakes can mimimise the risk of such issues becoming larger problems. Kaizen requires that we find out and address mistakes while they are still manageable. It might be tempting to overlook these problems until they become catastrophes. A successful company credits its achievements to the contributions of its people and the effectiveness of its institutional procedures. When things are not functioning optimally, there may be a reluctance to speak up. By glossing over the mistakes, businesses would lose chances to retain their focus and remain competitive. When employees report that there are no problems, a red flag should be raised. Steps should be taken to make improvements as necessary.

Develop New Services and Products

There is a common misconception that the incremental steps of Kaizen only yield marginal results, but these steps lead to breakthroughs that change the world over time. Contrary to belief, questioning isn't only driven by curiosity. It is an important skill and brings about one's creativity. Creativity is not sporadic; it is an activity that involves paying attention to the trivial moments of life. Creativity leads to successful services, products and changes. Though creativity can be practiced at any time, there are moments when ideas flourish. Some of those moments are:

a. **Wastefulness:** Instances when something is misplaced, time is wasted or items are damaged lead to anger and frustration. We need to reconsider our actions and by being curious, we can find solutions.

b. **Embarrassment:** Embarrassment is caused when there is a discrepancy between our actions and expectations. Some try to hide their mistakes while others own up to their mistakes and even laugh at the fact that they committed them and will move on as quickly as they can. In this state, creativity can manifest in the efforts of trying to cover up the mistake.

Kaizen presumes that human beings will make mistakes. Keep in mind that in an organisation, every individual is responsible. Rather than allowing mistakes as markers of failure, Kaizen improves your ability to detect and rectify such minor mistakes.

Kaizen insists that everyone in the company is highly responsible for quality and productivity to the same degree. Furthermore, it is the responsibility of the management to facilitate the smooth flow of suggestions and ideas from the lower managers to the top managers and throughout the department. These ideas and suggestions should clear pathways from bottom to top.

❑

8

QCD and Kaizen Goals

It is a universally acknowledged principle in a market economy that customers reign supreme; satisfying their expectations regarding the quality, cost, and timely delivery (QCD) of products and services is the ultimate goal that every business strives to achieve. This focal point on QCD is a direct consequence of the overarching Kaizen philosophy and its related activities, which are fundamentally geared towards the continuous improvement of these critical factors. Neglecting QCD can prove detrimental to the very survival of a business enterprise, thereby rendering it an indispensable top priority.

The pursuit of quality is a thread that runs through the entire lifecycle of a product or service, weaving through every stage from procurement to development, design, manufacturing, marketing, distribution, and after-sales support. As Masaaki Imai, a renowned expert on Kaizen, articulated, the inception of new products, services or processes commences with the creation of blueprints and accompanying documentation. This early phase presents a valuable window of opportunity to identify and rectify any potential malfunctions or deficiencies, a proactive approach that is significantly more cost-effective than attempting to address issues later in the cycle, which can incur substantial expenses.

Recognising the critical importance of this proactive approach, Japanese management embraced the Quality Function Deployment (QFD) methodology, also known as the Quality Assurance System diagram, as a potent tool to facilitate this endeavour. QFD enables organisations to systematically translate customer requirements into relevant technical specifications, ensuring that quality is built into the product or service from the outset, rather than being an afterthought.

In summary, the text underscores the pivotal role of customers in dictating business success, the centrality of QCD in achieving this success, the pervasive nature of quality across all stages of the product/service lifecycle, the advantages of addressing quality issues early in the development process, and the Japanese management's adoption of QFD as a structured approach to embedding quality into the core of their offerings.

While quality is paramount, cost-effectiveness is an equally crucial factor that determines an organisation's success. Cost-effectiveness encompasses the overall expenditure incurred throughout the entire lifecycle of a product or service, spanning design, production, sales and after-sales support. It is important to note that cost reduction is not merely about indiscriminate cost-cutting measures; rather, it is a nuanced exercise in cost management.

Dedicated cost management teams are tasked with overseeing the development, manufacture and sale of high-quality products or services while simultaneously minimising costs. How a product is designed, produced and brought to market can significantly influence the degree of resource waste, making it a critical consideration. The ultimate objective is to strike a delicate balance between improving quality and reducing costs, as this synergy is vital for organisational survival and growth.

Cost management encompasses a wide spectrum of activities, ranging from overall cost reduction in the workplace through the elimination of waste to cost planning strategies aimed at maximising the margin between revenue and expenditure. The elimination of waste, a cornerstone of cost reduction, can be achieved through the implementation of various waste elimination methods discussed earlier.

However, it is crucial to recognise that indiscriminate cost-cutting measures, such as restructuring, pressuring suppliers, or laying off employees, can disrupt the quality process and potentially lead to a deterioration in quality standards. Therefore, cost management must be a holistic endeavour that encompasses activities such as standardisation, policy deployment, education and training.

In the context of training, contemporary organisations often place excessive emphasis on the impartation of knowledge alone. In contrast, the Kaizen philosophy places great importance on the improvement of fundamental organisational values, which are cultivated through group learning environments. These values encompass self-discipline, common sense, economy and order, all of which are essential for fostering a culture of continuous improvement.

In essence, the passage highlights the importance of balancing quality and cost-effectiveness, the distinction between cost reduction and cost management, the role of dedicated teams in overseeing this balance, the potential consequences of indiscriminate cost-cutting measures, and the significance of fostering fundamental organisational values through group learning in the Kaizen approach.

The Elements for Successful Kaizen Applications

For Kaizen methodologies to be successfully implemented and yield sustained benefits, several critical elements must be meticulously addressed:

a. **Clearly defined and specific goals and objectives,** underpinned by a comprehensive and well-developed mandate that provides a solid foundation and direction for the initiative are paramount. This mandate should be communicated transparently, ensuring alignment across the organisation.

b. **Unwavering commitment from top management** is paramount. Leaders must not only embrace new ideas and philosophies but also actively drive rapid improvement throughout the organisation. Their visible sponsorship and embodiment of Kaizen principles are crucial for cultivating a culture of continuous improvement.

c. **Comprehensive training for teams** directly involved in the Kaizen initiative is essential. This involves imparting a deep understanding of the Kaizen philosophy, tools, techniques, and their practical applications, ensuring a shared knowledge base and skill set.

d. **Access to highly experienced and extensively trained facilitators** who can provide expert guidance throughout the assessment, event execution, and follow-up phases is crucial. These facilitators should possess a proven track record in leading successful Kaizen events and navigating potential challenges.

e. **An organisational commitment to meticulously follow through and sustain the improvements** achieved during the Kaizen initiative is crucial. This involves establishing robust mechanisms for monitoring progress, reinforcing new practices, and continuously refining processes to prevent backsliding.

9

Rewards and Recognition Functions of Kaizen

In corporate culture, three key components are corporate values, leadership, and the structure of rewards and recognition. The rewards system strongly reflects the organisation's democratic and innovative philosophy. It reinforces employee commitment to the corporate culture and values.

Rewards and Recognition (R&R) programmes are powerful tools for organisations striving to implement TQM. Some examples include:

1. **Gain Sharing Plans:** These schemes tie employee rewards directly to improvements in quality, productivity or cost savings achieved through Kaizen activities.

f. **The formation of a multidisciplinary team** that is well-balanced in terms of expertise, perspectives and skills is essential. This diversity fosters a holistic approach and ensures that momentum is maintained during and after the event, enabling the successful integration of improvements into daily operations.

g. **Clearly delineated roles and responsibilities for all participants**, including the team leader, process owner, Kaizen consultants, and co-leaders is important. Unambiguous role definitions prevent duplication of efforts, promote accountability, and ensure seamless coordination throughout the initiative's lifecycle. Successful Kaizen applications require a supportive organisational culture that encourages open communication, empowers employees to identify and address inefficiencies, and fosters a mindset of continuous learning and adaptation. Adequate resources, including time, budget and training provisions, must be allocated to support the implementation and long-term sustainability of Kaizen initiatives.

By addressing these elements comprehensively, organisations can create an environment conducive to the effective implementation of Kaizen methodologies, enabling them to realise substantial improvements in quality, efficiency and overall organisational performance while fostering a culture of continuous improvement.

❑

2. **Suggestion Systems:** Employees are recognised and rewarded (monetarily or non-monetarily) for their valuable process improvement ideas.

3. **Quality Awards/Bonuses:** Outstanding teams or individuals driving quality excellence through Kaizen efforts are publicly honoured.

4. **Public Recognition:** Simple acts of appreciation like posting success stories reinforce positive Kaizen behaviours.

5. **Promotion Opportunities:** Contributions to continuous improvement can be factored into advancement decisions.

An effective R&R programme demonstrates the management's commitment to quality values. By celebrating small wins and Kaizen mindsets, it motivates employees to actively participate in the never-ending improvement journey central to TQM. It aligns rewards with desired behaviours like problem-solving, teamwork and process optimisation.

Importantly, R&R is most impactful when coupled with empowerment—giving employees autonomy, resources and a blame-free environment to experiment with Kaizen initiatives. An enabling culture amplifies the power of R&R to sustain quality momentum.

R&R plays a crucial role in providing feedback, a major component of Kaizen. It indicates achievement and serves as a form of feedback on the results of team and individual efforts. Recognition communicates to team members that they are on the right track and making progress towards continuous improvement goals.

This feedback through recognition can come from various sources:

- Other teams within the organisation: Recognition from fellow employees fosters mutual appreciation and creates an environment where teams acknowledge each other's successes.
- Supervisors and managers: Acknowledgement from managers and supervisors reinforces desired Kaizen behaviours.
- External customers in the marketplace: Recognition from external customers affirms quality improvement, showing the organisation's commitment to customers.
- Internal customers across functions: Recognition of internal customers acknowledges the importance of cross-functional collaboration.

Receiving this positive feedback in the form of rewards and public recognition does more than just celebrate success. It validates that the Kaizen efforts and incremental improvements undertaken by teams and individuals are indeed moving the organisation in the right direction.

The feedback loop created by R&R programmes motivates participants to sustain their Kaizen mindset and maintain the cycle of never-ending improvements at the heart of the TQM/Kaizen philosophy. It builds confidence that their contributions are valued and impactful. In essence, integrating R&R acts as a powerful mechanism to provide the continuous encouragement, progress tracking, and course correction needed to fully institutionalise Kaizen as a cultural way of life throughout the organisation. R&R helps reinforce quality-related behaviours and achievements that align with the organisation's TQM goals. Positive reinforcement through R&R increases the likelihood that desired actions/mindsets will be repeated.

Different forms of public recognition demonstrate to internal and external stakeholders the success enjoyed by teams and individuals within the TQM framework. It showcases their sustained commitment to continuous improvement. R&R highlights exemplary employees and teams whose contributions propel the organisation forward on its quality journey. Recognition acts as a motivating factor that stimulates employees to expend more effort towards Kaizen activities. Being honoured for improvements, no matter how incremental, encourages participation and sustains the momentum of the never-ending improvement cycle.

In essence, a well-designed R&R programme does not just celebrate past successes. It reinforces the vital behaviours, mindsets and cross-functional collaboration needed to ingrain TQM/Kaizen as an encompassing management system. Public recognition validates organisational quality values and priorities. By consistently providing authentic, criteria-based positive reinforcement, R&R motivates the workforce to internalise and live those values daily through their process improvement efforts. It fosters a sense of shared ownership over quality outcomes.

R&R crystallises the cultural shift required to fully transition to a Kaizen-based, customer-focused operating philosophy that transcends just implementing TQM tools and techniques. It is a critical catalyst for individual and organisational transformation.

R&R visibly shows how the organisation values and appreciates the employees' efforts in embodying its core organisational values such as quality, continuous improvement, etc. The efforts are recognised, reinforcing the importance of employees in the organisation.

The R&R system increases awareness among the workforce that management is committed to rewarding those who seriously apply and embody essential TQM principles like continuous improvement, quality focus, and customer satisfaction.

Employees are greatly motivated to sustain their engagement and consistency in TQM/Kaizen practices when they see the R&R processes consistently implemented. They perceive the management's R&R initiatives as a genuine demonstration of the organisation's commitment to its stated quality values and philosophies. By frequently highlighting and celebrating progress, R&R programmes reinforce that TQM/Kaizen is not just a flavour-of-the-month programme, but a fundamental operating strategy. This awareness builds trust that efforts towards enhancing quality will be recognised and valued long-term.

Additionally, R&R criteria transparently communicate what behaviours and achievements are deemed exemplary by leadership. This clarity aligns employee efforts toward those recognised quality goals.

In essence, systematic R&R implementation signals organisational support and investments in TQM/Kaizen as a sustained competitive measure rather than a short-term cost-cutting exercise. This motivates employees to fully engage and take ownership as stakeholders in the quality journey. The processes of TQM and the Kaizen philosophy demand empowered and engaged team members, cross-functional collaboration, and employee involvement across the organisation. R&R programmes help motivate these various teams and individual contributors to continue actively participating in their respective roles and functions.

R&R fosters a positive environment where teams and individuals are motivated to engage in constructive competition and challenge each other to drive continuous improvement. This creates a win-win situation benefiting both employees and the organisation. Employees are motivated when they are recognised for utilising TQM tools (such as quality circles, process mapping, etc.) to solve problems, as well as for their interactions and collaborations with external customers and internal process partners.

By incentivising desired behaviours like cross-functional teamwork, customer focus, problem-solving skills, and effective use of quality management methodologies, R&R empowers employees at all levels to take ownership of the improvement process. The employees feel valued for contributing their ideas and expertise, which fosters a sense of empowerment.

This sense of empowerment catalyses participation in Kaizen activities and increases the organisational capability for ongoing, employee-driven improvement aligned with TQM principles. Effective R&R removes barriers to change and makes employees active stakeholders in the quality journey.

Thus, by recognising and rewarding behaviours that drive continuous improvement, R&R programmes not only motivate employees but foster a culture of excellence, which ensures that the organisation remains competitive.

❑

TMQ and Kaizen

Kaizen is an approach that encompasses various activities and initiatives like suggestion systems and TQM itself. TQM, also referred to as Total Quality Management, is a movement aimed at enhancing managerial performance at every organisational level. It deals with aspects such as quality assurance, employee engagement, safety, cost reduction, productivity improvement, and continuous enhancement.

In the TQM process, people play a pivotal role. It involves aspects such as training, teamwork, organisational culture, incentives, and involving employees in work. The TQM journey comprises cross-functional management of the organisation, organisational development, and deployment of quality practices throughout the organisation. TQM serves as both a tool and a concept for improving the overall performance of individuals within the organisation.

TQM integrates existing improvement efforts, fundamental management techniques, and technical tools into a disciplined approach aimed at continuously improving the organisation. The ultimate goal of these activities is to increase customer satisfaction. Although technical and mechanical aspects of improvement are necessary, it is essential to emphasise the roles and involvement of people in these processes.

In order to boost productivity, improve quality, and remain competitive, an enterprise needs to tap into the inherent potential of its workforce by empowering every employee to do their job accurately from the outset. Senior management should demonstrate their commitment to improving quality by continually pursuing such efforts along with every employee.

The organisation should provide an environment where employees voluntarily cooperate to achieve organisational objectives. Management should be open to ideas and contributions from employees, while also communicating their own ideas and goals. The TQM philosophy offers a holistic approach to improve organisational quality by examining work processes from an integrated, systematic, consistent, and organisation-wide perspective.

a. **Satisfying Customer Needs:** TQM is centred on meeting or exceeding the needs and expectations of both external customers who purchase the company's products/services, as well as internal customers—

the employees across different functions and levels. Understanding customer requirements and incorporating their feedback is vital for improving quality.

b. **Organisation-wide Involvement:** Effective TQM requires the active participation and collaboration of all units, departments and levels within the organisation. From the frontline employees to management, everyone must be involved in quality efforts in their respective roles and responsibilities. Cross-functional teamwork is encouraged.

c. **Understanding Process Variation:** A key aspect is recognising and managing variation that exists in all processes. Statistical methods are used to study this variation, identify its sources/causes, and implement improvements that reduce excessive variation, leading to more consistent and predictable processes.

d. **Continuous Kaizen:** Kaizen, or continuous incremental improvement, is a core tenet. TQM rejects the idea of one-time quality improvements. Instead, it promotes ongoing activities, no matter how small, that refine processes, reduce waste, and enhance quality standards incrementally over time.

e. **Employee Empowerment:** Perhaps most critically, TQM depends on the ideas, engagement, and motivation of all employees. It aims to create an environment where employees at all levels feel ownership, are empowered to identify improvement opportunities, and are recognised/rewarded for their contributions to boosting productivity and quality.

In essence, TQM takes a comprehensive, organisation-wide approach that aligns every function, process and individual towards the strategic goals of achieving superior quality and customer satisfaction through incremental, continuous efforts. However, impatience during the TQM implementation can lead to disappointment and frustration, as sustainable quality improvements require long-term commitment. Thus, patience and strong leadership are crucial for promoting and institutionalising TQM principles across the organisation.

It is clear that employee involvement at all levels and adopting a process-oriented approach to manufacturing operations are major cornerstones that underpin successful TQM efforts. The structure and activities of cross-functional teams are basic requirements for fostering individual participation and enhancing the organisation's ability to deploy quality processes consistently.

TQM, which drives continuous improvement in organisations, is analogous to the Kaizen philosophy of incremental, gradual enhancements. The characteristics and various elements of TQM and Kaizen are highly supportive of each other—both philosophies essentially mandate a unified organisational mindset and culture focused on never-ending refinement.

Achieving quality excellence through TQM is like a journey rather than reaching a destination. It requires steadfast patience from leaders, an engaged workforce centred around process discipline, and the cultivation of an organisational culture that embraces Kaizen as a way of life. When these cornerstones are firmly established, TQM and Kaizen become mutually reinforcing improvement paradigms, driving sustained excellence in any organisation.

Different types of teams play different roles in organisational dynamics. Here is an overview:

a. **Intact Workgroups:** These are permanent teams comprising employees responsible for ongoing operations or processes like production teams, sales teams, etc. They operate with clear roles, responsibilities and workflows.

b. **Problem-Solving Teams:** These are temporary teams formed to tackle a particular problem or issue and recommend solutions. They are disbanded once their objective is achieved. Examples include quality circles and task forces.

c. **Cross-Functional Teams:** These teams bring together people from various functions and departments to work on a specific objective requiring different skill sets and perspectives. They facilitate coordination across boundaries.

d. **Implementation and Proactive Teams:** Implementation teams are tasked with executing and managing a specific initiative or change effort. Proactive teams continuously identify and work on improvement opportunities before problems arise.

e. **Small Groups:** These are teams typically comprising 5-12 members working collaboratively. They include self-managed teams given autonomy over their work processes.

Regardless of type, effective teams generally exhibit some common characteristics:

- Clear goals/purpose aligned with organisational objectives
- Defined roles and responsibilities
- Mutual accountability and commitment
- Open communication and information sharing
- Valuing diverse perspectives
- Focus on collective performance, not just individual contributors

Fostering an organisation-wide culture that promotes proper team formation, empowerment and collaborative mindsets is critical for leveraging the potential of these team structures and ensuring the organisation's success.

❑

11

Group Activities

Small group activities originated in Japanese companies as a way to improve business processes and find solutions to organisational problems. Two prominent types of small groups are cross-functional teams and quality circles.

Cross-functional teams bring together employees from various departments and functional areas to work collaboratively on a specific objective or improvement opportunity that transcend organisational boundaries. The diverse skillsets and perspectives enables a more comprehensive analysis of processes and problems. These teams facilitate coordination and knowledge sharing across functions.

Quality circles, on the other hand, are small groups of employees, often from the same work area, who meet regularly to identify, analyse and solve work-related problems affecting their area. Using quality tools and structured techniques like root cause analysis, they develop and implement solutions. Quality circles empower front-line employees to enhance processes and drive incremental Kaizen improvements.

Both cross-functional teams and quality circles create a participatory environment where workers at all levels are engaged in continual improvement activities aligned with the philosophies of Total Quality Management (TQM) and Kaizen. Employees apply structured problem-solving methods to enhance quality, productivity, cost reduction and customer satisfaction.

After proving successful in Japanese companies, the concepts of cross-functional teams and quality circles have been adopted by organisations globally as powerful small group activities These approaches harness employee expertise and ingenuity in identifying improvement opportunities.

Cross-Functional Teams

These teams are formed specifically to conduct Kaizen events and continuous improvement initiatives. The team leader's primary focus is on facilitating how the diverse members work together as a team, rather than solely on the outputs they produce.

Even if a problem is confined to a single team member's domain initially, solutions are sought collaboratively as a team. This reflects the Kaizen philosophy's process-oriented approach of looking at the bigger picture.

The team leader acts as a coach, paying close attention to time management, maintaining discipline, encouraging participation and involvement from all members, enabling open communication, boosting team morale, and fostering skill development within the team.

The cross-functional team itself is responsible for attaining the targeted improvement results they set out to achieve. One key challenge is first properly scoping and defining the problem to tackle, as well as determining how to effectively measure the outcomes of their improvement efforts.

Overall, these teams harness the collective expertise and different perspectives across functions to holistically analyse processes, identify improvement opportunities, and implement Kaizen solutions in a collaborative manner under the coach's guidance.

Important rules and principles that cross-functional Kaizen teams should follow.

For the Kaizen approach to be effective, certain guidelines must be established for how cross-functional teams operate:

a. Contribution and participation from every team member is expected and encouraged. Diverse perspectives and active involvement from all functions is crucial.

b. The team must align on and commit to shared goals and objectives for the Kaizen initiative. A united vision prevents working at cross-purposes.

c. Conflicts and differing viewpoints among team members are negotiated and resolved through open discussion, rather than suppressed. The generation of better solutions should be through healthy conflict resolution.

d. Any criticism during Kaizen activities must be directed at the processes being analysed, not towards individual team members. This blame-free environment promotes psychological safety.

By adhering to these rules of engagement, cross-functional Kaizen teams can capitalise on their inherent diversity while avoiding dysfunctional team dynamics. Some key enablers that facilitate this process are:

- Mutual respect and valuing each member's contributions
- Establishing team decision-making processes upfront
- Empowering members to surface problems without fear
- Maintaining a constructive attitude focused on improvement

Effective coaching and facilitation are required to instil these ways of working that depart from traditional hierarchical management approaches. When implemented properly, these team norms build trust, shared ownership, and unleash the full creative problem-solving potential of the cross-functional Kaizen team.

a. Work teams have autonomy and control over functional responsibilities and the design/structure of work. This promotes ownership.

b. Optimal interface and interaction between team members and any equipment/technology they use is designed for maximum effectiveness.

c. Continuous development and training opportunities are viewed as long-term endeavours to build team capabilities over time.

d. Jobs are designed, and skills are developed, to ensure effective utilisation of all resources. This allows teams to quickly adapt to changing conditions.

e. Team rewards and recognition are directly linked to their contributions and overall effectiveness as a high-performing unit.

In addition to the previously mentioned principles, some more factors contribute to the success of Kaizen teams.

- Clear roles, responsibilities and decision-making processes defined within the team.
- Open communication channels enable knowledge sharing across functions.
- Performance metrics align with organisational goals and customer needs.
- Leadership provides an enabling environment of psychological safety.
- Teams are empowered to experiment and implement their Kaizen solutions.

By putting these factors in place, cross-functional teams can leverage their diverse strengths, rapidly respond to improvement opportunities, and sustain a high level of performance over time in driving continuous Kaizen activities throughout the organisation.

Quality Circles

A quality circle is a small group of employees who convene regularly, often daily, to discuss and work on quality-related problems impacting the organisation. These circles serve as a source of empowerment, allowing workers to directly identify and drive quality improvements. Adopting a quality circle entails both a task focus on continuous improvement as well as a social focus on team dynamics. To maximise effectiveness, commitment and buy-in are imperative at all levels, from senior leadership, unit managers to supervisors and the circle members themselves.

For quality circles to take ownership of testing and piloting solutions, they require allocated budgets and resources. Structured approaches are needed for comprehensively analysing problems, defining the core issues, and understanding the relationships between various components. This involves using both quantitative measurement techniques as well as qualitative assessments based on the experience and judgement of circle members. Properly scoping and verifying the actual root causes of problems is critical before developing countermeasures.

Quality circles must also assess whether the problems are continuous/recurring or one-off issues to determine appropriate solutions. Having a shared understanding of the problem's impact on processes, quality, productivity and other factors is essential.

Initially, quality circles were considered crucial to Japan's achievements. While there were numerous success stories, some companies continued utilising them, while others viewed them as unsuccessful endeavours. The reasons behind their failures were as follows:

a. Insufficient training on tools designed for problem-solving

b. Inadequate evaluation and measurement of outcomes

c. Team members lacking expertise or ill-suited for addressing the problem at hand

d. Lack of comprehension of the process by management

e. Excessive control and dominance of the process by management.

In essence, the text highlights that while quality circles initially contributed to Japan's success, their effectiveness diminished due to factors such as lack of proper training, inadequate result measurement, inappropriate team composition, and management's lack of understanding or excessive control over the process.

Quality circle teams, also known as Process Improvement Teams (PIT) or Quality Improvement Teams (QIT), are integral to both public and private sector organisations. For these teams to be effective, the entire management of the organisation must believe in the team process, consider the proposals put forth, and facilitate the implementation of feasible solutions, from pilot stages to full-scale operation. A crucial factor contributing to the success of quality service teams is a willingness to avoid obstruction and maintain an open mindset. Embracing the philosophy that experiments foster learning is highly beneficial, acknowledging that trials and experiments can lead to valuable insights and improvements.

In summary, the text emphasises the need for organisation-wide support, receptiveness to proposals, facilitation of feasible solutions, an unobstructed and open-minded approach, and a recognition that experimentation aids the learning process for quality circle teams to thrive and drive improvement within organisations.

❑

Measurement of Kaizen Effect

The concept of Gross Domestic Product (GDP) represents the total value-added produced within a country over a specific period. Notably, a nation's economic growth rate is directly correlated with the rate of increase in its total value-added. In this context, the philosophy of Kaizen, emphasising continuous improvement, can positively impact various aspects of business performance, including profits and sales.

However, the effects of Kaizen are not always immediately apparent in the short-term improvement of business performance metrics. This is because the value-added generated by a company is the cumulative result of every activity within the organisation, of which Kaizen constitutes only a part. Therefore, it would be unreasonable to attribute every increase in value-added solely to Kaizen initiatives. A more prudent approach is to assess the effects of Kaizen on an activity-by-activity basis.

It is worth noting that some of the effects of Kaizen cannot be quantitatively measured, as they may be qualitative in nature. Nevertheless, for those effects that can be quantified, some may be reflected in economic terms, while others may not have a direct monetary value associated with them.

To evaluate the impact of Kaizen comprehensively, it is recommended to employ a combination of quantitative measurement indices and monetary valuations. The effects of Kaizen can be categorised into four broad categories: qualitative, quantitative, economic, and non-economic.

- **Qualitative effects** may include improvements in areas such as employee morale, customer satisfaction, or organisational culture, which can be challenging to quantify but can significantly contribute to long-term success.
- **Quantitative effects** encompass measurable improvements in areas such as productivity, cycle times, defect rates, or inventory levels, which can be tracked and analysed using relevant metrics.
- **Economic effects** refer to the direct financial impacts of Kaizen initiatives, such as cost savings, revenue growth, or profitability improvements, which can be quantified in monetary terms.
- **Non-economic effects** may include intangible benefits such as enhanced brand reputation, improved regulatory compliance, or increased environmental sustainability, which may not directly translate into monetary value but can contribute to long-term organisational success.

By evaluating the effects of Kaizen a
four categories, organisations can gain a com
understanding of the value-added generated
continuous improvement efforts, enabling then
informed decisions and allocate resources effe
sustain and amplify the benefits of Kaizen over ti

a. **Qualitative Effects**: These are improvement be observed and experienced, but cannot be q or measured numerically. Examples include employee morale, improved organisational increased customer satisfaction, and better te and communication.

b. **Quantitative Effects**: Quantitative effects r improvements that can be measured and expresse numerical data or metrics. These include reduct defect rates, cycle time improvements, produ gains, inventory level reductions, or increases in c

c. **Economic Effects**: Economic effects are a sub quantitative effects that can be directly translate monetary terms, impacting the financial perform of the organisation. There are two types of econ effects:

1. *Actualised Economic Effects:* These are econo benefits that have a tangible and realised im on the value-added generated by the compa Examples include cost savings from proc improvements, revenue increases from high

productivity, or profitability gains from waste reduction.

2. *Proforma Economic Effects:* These are economic effects that do not directly impact the company's value-added, unlike actualised economic effects. They may represent potential future benefits or hypothetical scenarios rather than realised gains.

d. **Non-Economic Effects**: Non-economic effects are quantitative improvements that can be measured numerically but cannot be directly expressed in monetary terms. Examples include reductions in lead times, improvements in on-time delivery rates, or decreases in energy consumption or carbon footprint.

In this context, the definition of value-added is considered to be the net sales revenue generated by the company, excluding outsourcing costs. Alternatively, it can be viewed as the sum of the company's capital gains and labour costs.

While economic effects directly impact financial performance, the qualitative, quantitative and non-economic effects also contribute significantly to the long-term success and competitiveness of the organisation, even if their impact is not immediately reflected in monetary terms.

1. **Evaluation Targets:** The evaluation indices consist of not only achievement indices (actual effects) but also those that measure changes in employee behaviour and the work environment, including activity and environment indices (such as safety). The reasons for this comprehensive approach are:

(a) In addition to actual effects, Kaizen places significant importance on awareness, human resource development, and changes in employee behaviour within the organisation.

(b) It aims to improve work safety and the overall work environment.

(c) Quantitative and actual effects may take time to become observable, especially when significant time and effort are required to improve the work environment and management systems before addressing specific problems.

(d) Qualitative effects are often realised before quantitative effects, and thus should not be underestimated.

2. **Evaluation Indices:** Evaluation indices consist of raw data that can be directly measured, such as time durations, frequencies, or counts, as well as processed data derived from multiple raw data points. In some companies, operators are responsible for recording and measuring raw data, which managers and supervisors then use to calculate the effects.

Kaizen consulting services are often provided to companies that cannot measure and record data essential for proper production management. In such cases, quantitative effects may be difficult to measure due to a lack of information on the company's pre-Kaizen conditions.

To prevent this, Kaizen trainers must collect important data and information during corporate diagnosis and obtain any missing information during the Kaizen guidance process. Establishing systems to collect and measure essential data should be an integral part of Kaizen activities within different companies.

Some environment and activity indices include those used to measure 5S (Sort, Set in order, Shine, Standardise, Sustain) practices and the level of Kaizen activity related to morale and work safety.

By comprehensively evaluating both achievement indices and changes in behaviour, work environment, and activity levels, organisations can gain a holistic understanding of the impact of Kaizen initiatives, enabling them to make informed decisions and continuously improve their processes and systems.

Raw Materials Monitoring

For raw materials that are not monitored on a daily basis, it is essential for operators and field supervisors to measure and record the relevant data before and after the implementation of Kaizen initiatives. This baseline data is crucial for accurately assessing the effects of Kaizen on raw material usage and efficiency. By establishing this baseline, organisations can effectively track improvements resulting from Kaizen interventions.

Delayed Effects

It is crucial to note that the effects of Kaizen may not always be immediately apparent during the process or activity where the Kaizen initiative is implemented. In some cases, the benefits may become evident at a later stage or in other areas of the organisation's operations. This emphasises the need for comprehensive and ongoing monitoring, as well as a holistic perspective when evaluating the impact of Kaizen across different processes and departments.

By incorporating raw material monitoring by frontline personnel and recognising the potential for delayed or indirect effects, organisations can better capture the full extent of improvements resulting from Kaizen initiatives. This data-driven approach, combined with a broad viewpoint, enables a more accurate assessment of the qualitative, quantitative, economic and non-economic effects of continuous improvement efforts.

It is also worth noting that Kaizen is an ongoing process, and its effects may continue to compound over time as the culture of continuous improvement becomes ingrained within the organisation. Consistent measurement, evaluation, and adaptation are essential to sustaining and amplifying the benefits of Kaizen in the long run.

❑

How Kaizen Affects Nutritional Habits?

Utilising Kaizen methods in your dietary habits can offer significant benefits to individuals seeking to transform their relationship with food. Rather than imposing strict limitations or sacrificing the enjoyment of food, endeavour to introduce gradual adjustments to your eating and drinking patterns, fostering a positive outlook on nourishing both your body and mind. Let's explore how Kaizen can reshape your dietary routines across three distinct timeframes: short, medium, and long-term objectives.

Increase Water Intake

The amount of water you consume daily should be tailored to factors such as your gender, dietary intake, physical activity level, and environmental conditions. While incorporating beverages like milk, coffee, tea, and sugar-free drinks, it's essential to prioritise water consumption. Initially, remembering to drink water consistently may pose challenges. However, through the gradual implementation of Kaizen principles, it can evolve into a routine with numerous benefits for the body. Stay attentive to your body's signals of thirst and ensure regular hydration. Avoid excessive hydration, as it can pose risks to your health.

Transition to Veganism

In today's society, meat consumption is widespread. However, reducing meat intake offers numerous proven health benefits. Kaizen serves as an effective tool for facilitating this transition, making it a gradual and manageable process. Emphasising the consumption of fruits and vegetables aligns with the dietary practices commonly observed in Japanese culture, promoting a cost-effective diet rich in essential nutrients found across various food groups. Implementing Kaizen principles can aid in gradually integrating more fruits and vegetables into your meals.

As you transition to a vegan lifestyle, it's crucial to limit sugar consumption. Excessive sugar intake, especially from soda drinks, is widely recognised as detrimental to health. While natural sugars in fruits are acceptable, Kaizen encourages a gradual reduction in overall sugar intake. Avoiding cereals with hidden sugars and gradually reducing sugar added to hot beverages are practical steps in this process.

Manage Food Portions

Controlling food portions involves reducing the quantity of food consumed. Several strategies can facilitate this reduction. Start by measuring your food servings to ensure accurate portions. Utilising smaller bowls and plates can trick the brain into perceiving larger portions. Avoid eating leftovers after meals. Also, pay attention to hunger cues and stop eating when you are satisfied..

Practice Mindful Eating

When eating, focus your attention on each bite and savour it fully. Appreciate the flavour and texture of food. Aim to eat in a setting with minimal distractions, such as at a table. Pay close attention to the preparation of your meals by choosing fresh ingredients. Enjoy the cooking process. This helps to have a deeper appreciation for food.

For long-term objectives, it's essential to cultivate mindfulness regarding your attitude towards food, its preparation, and the way it nourishes you. This transformation will unfold gradually, integrating seamlessly into your existing routine to ensure a lasting impact. As you reach milestones along this journey, monitor your progress and acknowledge your achievements with appropriate rewards.

To facilitate weight loss and promote healthier eating habits, managers can offer practical suggestions to employees within the organisation. Some of these suggestions include:

Opt for the children's meal when dining out, as the portion sizes are typically smaller than adult meals.

Slow down your eating pace, especially when consuming sweets, to fully savour and enjoy each bite. Pause between bites to enhance satisfaction.

Replace your usual morning muffin, bagel, or doughnut with toast or cereal to potentially lose up to 20 pounds annually.

Increase your daily water intake without changing your diet; keep a water bottle handy as a reminder to stay hydrated wherever you go.

Use smaller plates to trick your mind into feeling full with smaller portions, minimising leftovers and promoting a sense of satiety.

Request to have half of your meal boxed up before it's served, allowing you to enjoy a more appropriate portion size and prevent overeating.

Incorporate mind sculpting exercises into your daily routine to retrain your eating habits. Visualise yourself dining in a restaurant, eating slowly, drinking water, engaging in conversation, and leaving food on your plate. Add a new exercise each week to gradually reduce food portions without conscious effort.

Instead of turning to food for comfort when upset, experiment with alternative self-soothing techniques. Try journaling, increasing water intake, brief exercises, slow breathing, or reaching out to a friend for support.

Take a plastic bag with you when dining out and discreetly stash away bread to avoid temptation. Some believe that bread contributes to weight gain.

Lack of sleep triggers the release of hormones like ghrelin and leptin, which affect carbohydrate cravings. Gradually adjust your bedtime by going to bed a minute earlier each night, practicing slow breathing or reading before sleep. Increase this adjustment weekly until you feel more energetic and less sleepy upon waking.

Once you've built momentum, consider implementing email reminders to reinforce healthy habits. These reminders can encourage increased consumption of fruits and vegetables, participation in physical activities, reduction of saturated fats and sugar intake,. and more. Additionally, include practical suggestions such as taking walks during office breaks or opting for a salad with chicken for lunch.

As a manager, lead by example rather than merely advising your employees on healthy behaviours. Take actions like using the stairs instead of the elevator or escalator, practicing portion control, keeping healthy snacks at your desk, and displaying a wellness chart reflecting your daily healthy choices on your office wall.

To burn extra calories, consider these suggestions:

Take the stairs or walk up and down the escalator instead of riding.

Incorporate pushups into your daily routine, starting with five and gradually increasing by one each day.

Take regular breaks during work every 90 minutes to stroll around the office or engage in stretching exercises.

Stand or pace while on the phone or when brainstorming.

When travelling with wheeled luggage, carry it part of the time to add resistance and burn more calories.

❑

14

Use Kaizen to Improve Sleep

Optimising your sleep environment is a vital first step in applying Kaizen principles to enhance your sleep quality. Your bedroom should be a tranquil sanctuary, free from clutter, distractions, and external disruptions. Creating this calm and relaxing space sets the foundation for good sleep hygiene. Once you have established a serene sleep environment, you can then focus on implementing incremental changes to further refine your sleep routine. The Kaizen philosophy encourages making small, sustainable adjustments and evaluating their impact before introducing additional improvements.

- **De-cluttering:** Remove any unnecessary items or sources of visual clutter from your bedroom. A tidy and organised space can promote a sense of peace and relaxation, conducive to restful sleep.

- **Fresh Bedding:** Change your bed sheets regularly, at least once every two weeks. Clean, fresh bedding can improve comfort and create a more inviting sleep environment.
- **Noise Reduction:** Eliminate external noise sources as much as possible. Consider using earplugs, white noise machines, or soundproofing measures to create a quieter sleep sanctuary.
- **Soothing Sounds:** Incorporate calming, relaxing music or nature sounds played at a low volume. This can help mask any remaining ambient noise and promote a sense of tranquillity.
- **Light Control:** Ensure your bedroom is dark and cool by using blackout curtains or an eye mask to block out any external light sources. Optimal light and temperature levels can positively impact sleep quality.
- **Pleasant Aromas:** Surround yourself with pleasant, natural scents that you find calming and relaxing. Essential oils or aromatherapy can enhance the sensory experience of your sleep environment.
- **Digital Detox:** Turn off all electronic devices, including your phone, and block out any potential digital distractions or notifications. This practice promotes a true disconnect and allows your mind to unwind.
- **Reading:** Incorporate a relaxing pre-sleep routine, such as reading a physical book or engaging in light

stretching or meditation. These activities can signal to your body that it's time to wind down.

- **Self-Compassion:** Practice self-kindness and avoid berating yourself if you experience difficulties falling asleep. Approach the process with patience and a positive mindset, recognising that progress takes time and consistency.

By implementing these Kaizen-inspired adjustments gradually and consistently, you can cultivate an environment and routine that promotes optimal sleep quality. Remember to celebrate small victories, reflect on your progress, and continue refining your approach through ongoing experimentation and self-awareness.

Prioritising good sleep not only improves your overall well-being but also enhances your productivity, focus, and ability to engage in other areas of continuous improvement throughout your waking hours. Optimise your sleep environment, incorporating simple exercises into your routine can be highly beneficial for achieving a calm and relaxed state, conducive to restful sleep. Physical activity not only tires the body but can also have a profound effect on quieting the mind.

One such exercise that can be easily performed anywhere is alternate nostril breathing, also known as '*Nadi Shodhana Pranayama*' (नाड़ी शोधन प्राणायाम). This ancient yogic practice is renowned for its ability to promote relaxation and induce a sense of tranquility. Let's learn how to practice it.

- **Step-1:** Find a comfortable position, either sitting upright or lying down, that allows you to breathe freely and deeply.
- **Step-2:** Relax your entire body and gently close your eyes. Visualise your eyeballs floating peacefully in a cool pool of water, letting go of any tension or strain.
- **Step-3:** Using your left hand, close your left nostril with your thumb. Rest the second and third fingers of the same hand in your palm, extending the fourth and fifth fingers.
- **Step-4:** Inhale deeply through your right nostril, allowing the breath to fill your lungs. Then, close your right nostril with the fourth finger of your left hand while simultaneously releasing your thumb from your left nostril. Exhale slowly and completely through your left nostril.
- **Step-5:** Regulate your breathing, maintaining a steady and controlled rhythm. Repeat this alternating pattern of inhaling through one nostril and exhaling through the other for several minutes, allowing your breath to become progressively slower and more relaxed. As you continue this practice, you may notice a sense of calm washing over your mind and body. The alternating breath pattern can help soothe and balance the neural pathways, reducing mental agitation and promoting a state of relaxation.

- **Step-6:** After a few minutes, switch hands and repeat the exercise, this time closing your right nostril with your right thumb and breathing through your left nostril.

This simple yet powerful exercise can be incorporated into your pre-sleep routine or practiced whenever you feel the need to calm your mind and prepare your body for restful slumber. Remember, consistency and patience are essential when adopting new habits, so approach this practice with a mindset of continuous improvement, adjusting as needed to find the optimal routine for your unique needs. By combining a tranquil sleep environment with relaxation techniques like alternate nostril breathing, you are actively applying the principles of Kaizen to enhance your overall sleep quality, one small step at a time.

Good Morning Habits

The Kaizen philosophy emphasises the power of small, incremental changes to achieve continuous improvement. By applying this mindset to your morning routine, you can gradually develop habits that start your day on a positive and productive note.

- **Progressive Wake-Up Time:** Begin by setting your alarm just five minutes earlier than your usual wake-up time. This small adjustment can provide a sense of accomplishment and set the tone for further habit formation. Gradually increase this buffer until you reach your desired wake-up time, allowing your body and mind to adapt gradually.

- **Eliminating Morning Stressors:** Identify the sources of stress or friction in your current morning routine. Perhaps it's a cluttered environment, a lack of preparation the night before, or a chaotic schedule. Once you've pinpointed these stressors, brainstorm and implement simple solutions to eliminate or minimise them one by one.
- **Morning Exercise:** Incorporate a short, low-impact exercise routine into your mornings. This could be as simple as a few stretches, a brief yoga sequence, or a brisk walk around the block. Physical activity in the morning can energise you, boost your mood, and improve focus throughout the day.
- **Breathing Exercises:** Upon waking, take a few moments to practice deep breathing exercises. This simple act can help calm your mind, reduce anxiety, and promote a sense of tranquility as you start your day. Techniques like alternate nostril breathing or simple diaphragmatic breathing can be highly effective.
- **Hydration:** Make it a habit to drink a glass of water as soon as you wake up. Proper hydration is essential for overall well-being and can aid in digestion, cognitive function, and energy levels throughout the day.
- **Prioritise Breakfast:** Instead of rushing out the door, make time for a nutritious breakfast. Fuel your body with a balanced meal to kickstart your metabolism, provide sustained energy, and improve concentration.

By implementing these Kaizen-inspired adjustments gradually and consistently, you'll cultivate a morning routine that sets you up for success. Celebrate each small victory, reflect on your progress, and continue refining your approach through ongoing experimentation and self-awareness. The key to lasting habit change is to start small, be patient, and embrace the journey of continuous improvement. With time and persistence, these morning habits will become second nature, allowing you to begin each day with a sense of calm, focus and energy.

Improve Productivity

Japanese Zen practices, rooted in Zen Buddhism, offer a philosophical foundation to bring order, joy and a sense of purpose to one's life. Kaizen, with its emphasis on continuous improvement through small, incremental changes, can be a powerful tool for enhancing productivity and efficiency in both personal and professional contexts.

- **Identifying and Eliminating Waste:** The first step in the Kaizen approach to productivity is to identify areas where time and energy are being wasted or underutilised. This can be accomplished by tracking and analysing your daily activities, periods of downtime, and interruptions over the course of a week. By gaining this self-awareness, you can pinpoint unnecessary time-wasters and seek opportunities for optimisation. Additionally, evaluate routine tasks and consider applying standardisation techniques to streamline processes and eliminate redundancies.

- **Breaking Down Tasks:** Oftentimes, large or complex tasks can feel overwhelming, leading to procrastination or a lack of motivation. Kaizen encourages breaking down these tasks into smaller, more manageable components. By tackling one small step at a time, the overall goal becomes less daunting, and progress is more tangible, reducing stress and increasing a sense of accomplishment.
- **Continuous Evaluation and Adaptation:** Embrace a mindset of continuous learning and adaptation. Regularly evaluate which strategies, techniques, or routines are working effectively for you and which ones are hindering your productivity. Instead of clinging to ineffective methods, be willing to let go and focus your efforts on areas where you can make meaningful improvements. Solicit feedback, experiment with new approaches, and remain open to refining your processes based on your experiences.

Productivity is not a destination but an ongoing journey of refinement and self-awareness. By embracing the Kaizen philosophy, it's essential to cultivate a supportive environment that promotes productivity. This may involve minimising distractions, optimising your workspace, and prioritising self-care practices such as adequate rest, hydration, and regular breaks to prevent burnout.

You can continuously identify areas for improvement, implement incremental changes, and celebrate small victories along the way. This iterative approach not only enhances efficiency but also fosters a growth mindset and a sense of personal accountability, ultimately leading to a more fulfilling and purposeful life.

❑

15

Studying and Kaizen

The philosophy of Kaizen, with its emphasis on continuous improvement through small, incremental changes, can be effectively applied to the realm of studying and learning. Just as Kaizen drives organisational excellence, it can also empower individuals to enhance their academic performance and learning capabilities steadily over time. At the core of applying Kaizen to studying lies the mindset shift from viewing learning as a finite endeavour to embracing it as a lifelong journey of continuous growth and self-betterment. This mindset encourages students to approach their studies with a growth mindset, recognising that their abilities are not fixed but can be developed through consistent effort, strategic adjustments, and a willingness to learn from failures or setbacks.

One of the key principles of Kaizen is the identification and elimination of waste or inefficiencies, known as *muda* in Japanese. In the context of studying, this translates to identifying and addressing factors that hinder effective learning, such as procrastination, distractions, inefficient study techniques, or gaps in foundational knowledge. By systematically identifying and addressing these hindrances, students can streamline their learning process and optimise their time and effort.

Kaizen emphasises the importance of standardisation and the establishment of routines or processes that facilitate consistent performance. For students, this could involve developing structured study schedules, implementing effective note-taking strategies, or adopting proven techniques for information retention and recall. By standardising these practices, students can create a solid foundation upon which they can continuously refine and improve their methods. Furthermore, Kaizen encourages the practice of regularly reflecting on one's progress, identifying areas for improvement, and implementing small adjustments or experiments to enhance learning outcomes. This iterative cycle of feedback, analysis and adaptation allows students to tailor their approach to their unique learning styles, strengths and weaknesses, maximising their potential for academic success.

Collaboration and knowledge sharing are also integral components of Kaizen, and these principles can be applied to study groups or peer-to-peer learning environments. By fostering an open exchange of ideas, techniques and experiences, students can learn from one another, identify best practices, and collectively contribute to a culture of continuous improvement in their academic pursuits.

Additionally, the Kaizen philosophy emphasises the importance of developing a growth mindset and cultivating a sense of personal responsibility and ownership over one's learning journey. This mindset empowers students to take an active role in their education, embrace challenges as opportunities for growth, and persist in the face of obstacles or setbacks. By embracing the principles of Kaizen in their studying and learning endeavours, students can unlock a pathway to sustained academic excellence, personal growth, and the development of lifelong learning habits that will serve them well beyond their formal education.

Find Out How Best You Work

Discovering and leveraging your optimal study methods is a critical step in applying Kaizen principles to enhance your learning journey. Every individual has unique preferences, strengths and inclinations when it comes to acquiring and retaining information effectively. Thus, it is essential to experiment with various study techniques to identify the approach that resonates best with your personal learning style.

Some individuals may thrive by meticulously transcribing information from textbooks and then re-reading their notes for memorisation purposes. Others may lean more towards visual learning, preferring to create mental imagery or pictorial representations of concepts. Yet others may find that repetitive writing or rewriting of key points aids in solidifying their understanding and retention. Rather than attempting to emulate the study methods of others, which may not align with your unique cognitive processes, it is advisable to embark on a self-discovery journey. Allocate time to explore different techniques, assess their effectiveness for your learning needs, and gradually refine your approach based on your experiences and introspections.

Additionally, it is crucial to consider and cultivate an environment that fosters your optimal productivity and focus. Some individuals may perform best in complete silence, while others may benefit from the stimulation of background music or ambient sounds. Identifying the environmental conditions that enhance your concentration and energy levels can significantly boost the efficacy of your study sessions.

Once you have identified your preferred study techniques and optimal learning environment, the next step is to build a consistent routine that capitalises on these insights. By structuring your study sessions around your personal strengths and preferences, you can maximise the efficiency of your time investment and increase the likelihood of retaining and internalising the material effectively.

Embracing this self-awareness and tailoring your study approach to your unique learning profile exemplifies the Kaizen principle of continuous improvement through small, incremental adjustments. As you consistently refine and optimise your study methods, you will experience a compounding effect on your academic performance, cultivating a virtuous cycle of growth and self-betterment.

Effective Time Management

Individuals possess varying capacities for sustained focus and concentration during study sessions. While some may be able to maintain productivity over extended periods, such as ١٤ hours in a library setting, others may find waning attention and motivation after a certain duration. It is essential to understand your personal limits and patterns of productivity.

Experiment with different study durations and intervals, and identify the optimal time frames that allow you to maintain high levels of engagement and retention. For some, shorter bursts of intense focus followed by brief breaks may prove more effective than attempting to power through for hours on end.

Consider your personal chronobiology—the times of day when you experience peak mental alertness and energy levels. By aligning your study routine with your most productive hours, whether in the early morning, midday, or late evening, you can maximise the efficiency of your efforts.

Incorporating Breaks

Prolonged periods of intense study can lead to mental fatigue, diminished concentration, and a decline in overall productivity. To counteract this, it is crucial to incorporate regular breaks into your study routine. The famous adage 'the body is not firewood' highlights the importance of allowing your mind and body to rejuvenate periodically.

Consider implementing the Pomodoro Technique or similar time-management strategies that involve short bursts of focused work followed by brief respites. During these breaks, engage in activities that facilitate mental refreshment and physical rejuvenation, such as taking a short walk, practicing light stretches, or consuming hydrating beverages or healthy snacks.

These intermittent breaks not only help in maintaining concentration and motivation but also promote overall well-being by preventing burnout and allowing your mind to assimilate the information more effectively. By implementing effective time management strategies and incorporating regular breaks, you align with the Kaizen principles of continuous improvement and efficiency optimisation. This approach enables you to work smarter, not harder, and maximises the overall productivity and retention of your study sessions. Remember, the journey of learning is a marathon, not a sprint. By prioritising self-care and adopting a sustainable pace, you can cultivate a lifelong habit of continuous learning and growth, consistently enhancing your academic performance and personal development.

Setting Priorities

Identifying and prioritising areas of weakness or knowledge gaps is a crucial first step in the continuous improvement journey. It requires an honest self-assessment and a willingness to confront personal limitations without judgement or discouragement. This self-awareness lays the foundation for targeted growth and development.

Once you have identified your weaknesses or areas that require additional attention, the next step is to prioritise them based on factors such as their impact on your overall academic performance, the prerequisite nature of certain concepts for advanced learning, or the weight they carry in your course or program requirements.

The Kaizen approach encourages breaking down larger goals or challenges into manageable, incremental steps. By focusing on one weak area at a time, you can concentrate your efforts and resources more effectively, increasing the likelihood of mastering the material before moving on to the next priority. It is essential to establish specific, measurable, achievable, relevant, and time-bound (SMART) goals for each priority area. These goals serve as milestones along your continuous improvement journey, providing a sense of direction, motivation, and a means to track your progress.

While addressing your priorities, remain open to adjusting your approach based on feedback and self-reflection. Kaizen emphasises the importance of continuous refinement and adaptation, encouraging you to experiment with different study techniques, seek guidance from instructors or peers, and iterate until you find the most effective strategies for your unique learning needs.

The process of setting priorities and addressing weaknesses is not a one-time endeavour but rather an ongoing cycle of self-evaluation, goal-setting, implementation, and reassessment. Embrace this iterative approach as a lifelong habit, continuously identifying areas for growth and taking incremental steps toward mastery. By aligning your study efforts with your priorities and employing a structured, adaptive approach, you not only enhance your academic performance but also cultivate invaluable skills in self-discipline, time management, and a growth mindset—qualities that will serve you well beyond your academic pursuits.

Meticulous Note-Taking and Reference Tracking

As you delve into your studies, it is crucial to maintain a comprehensive and organised record of all the materials you reference, including page numbers, citations and sources. This practice not only aids in effective information retrieval and review but also fosters academic integrity by ensuring proper attribution of ideas and concepts.

Develop a consistent system for note-taking, whether digital or handwritten, that allows you to easily cross-reference and locate specific information when needed. Additionally, consider implementing techniques such as colour-coding, mind-mapping, or utilising note-taking software to enhance the organisation and accessibility of your study materials.

Studying in a Stimulating Environment

The physical environment in which you study can significantly impact your motivation, focus, and overall productivity. Experiment with different study spaces that stimulate your senses and provide an atmosphere conducive to learning.

For some, this may involve studying in a quiet library or dedicated study room; for others, a lively coffee shop or an outdoor setting with natural elements may prove more invigorating. Identify the environmental factors that help you maintain a state of focused attention and promote a positive mindset towards learning.

Goal-Setting and Visualisation

Establishing clear and specific goals is a fundamental principle of Kaizen, as it provides direction and a sense of purpose to your efforts. Before embarking on your study sessions, take the time to define your objectives, whether they are mastering a particular concept, completing a specific assignment, or achieving a desired grade. Furthermore, visualise yourself successfully attaining these goals, creating a mental image of the desired outcome. This practice not only reinforces your commitment but also helps to cultivate a growth mindset, promoting perseverance and resilience in the face of challenges.

Progress Tracking

Regularly monitoring and evaluating your progress is essential for maintaining motivation and identifying areas that require further attention or adjustment. Implement a system for tracking your achievements, whether through a dedicated journal, a digital app, or a simple checklist. Celebrate milestones, no matter how small, as they represent tangible evidence of your continuous improvement journey. Additionally, periodically reflect on your progress, analysing what strategies or techniques have proven effective and what areas may require modification or refinement.

Daily Planning and Time Management

Effective time management is a critical component of successful studying. Begin each day by creating a structured plan that allocates dedicated time for your study sessions, breaks, and other commitments. Prioritise your tasks based on their importance and urgency, and be realistic in your time estimations to avoid overburdening yourself. Remember, the Kaizen philosophy emphasises gradual improvement, so start with manageable goals and adjust as needed based on your progress and capacity. By incorporating these strategies into your study routine, you align with the principles of Kaizen, fostering a mindset of continuous improvement, self-awareness, and adaptability. Embrace this journey as a lifelong pursuit, continuously refining your approaches and celebrating each small step towards academic excellence and personal growth.

❑

The PDCA Cycle

The PDCA cycle is highly relevant to the practice of Kaizen, which is the philosophy of continuous improvement. The PDCA cycle is a continuous loop, emphasising the idea of ongoing improvement. Once the Act stage is completed, the cycle starts over again with a new Plan phase, aiming to further refine and optimise the process.

The PDCA cycle is a powerful tool in Kaizen because it provides a structured approach to identifying opportunities for improvement, implementing changes, evaluating their effectiveness, and making necessary adjustments. By following this cycle, organisations can foster a culture of continuous improvement and achieve incremental, sustainable progress over time.

The PDCA cycle provides a powerful framework for implementing the Kaizen philosophy of continuous improvement. Its emphasis on structured planning, evaluation and adjustment aligns with the core principles of Kaizen, making it an essential tool for organisations seeking to embrace a culture of incremental progress and eliminate waste. The PDCA cycle is a fundamental concept in the Kaizen philosophy and is used as a model for continuous improvement. PDCA stands for Plan-Do-Check-Act, and it is an iterative four-step management method used for the control and continuous improvement of processes and products.

The four steps in the PDCA Cycle

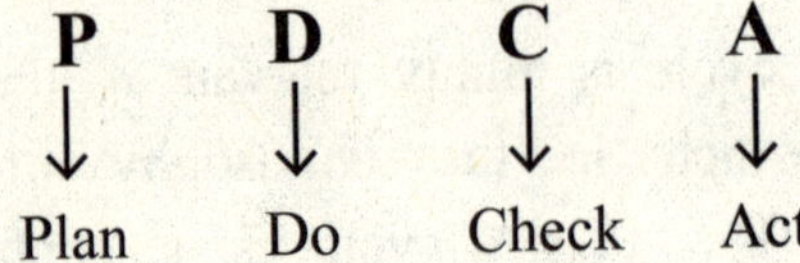

Plan

In this step, you identify and analyse the problem or opportunity for improvement, gather relevant data, and develop a plan of action. This involves setting goals, defining measures, and determining the necessary steps to achieve the desired improvement.

Do

This step involves implementing the plan developed in the previous stage. It involves executing the planned changes, often on a small scale or as a pilot, to test the effectiveness of the solution.

Check

After implementing the changes, this step involves monitoring and evaluating the results. Data is collected and analysed to determine whether the changes led to the desired improvement. The results are compared to the goals set in the planning stage.

Act

Based on the evaluation in the previous step, actions are taken to either adopt, adjust, or abandon the changes. If the changes are successful, they are standardised and incorporated into the regular process. If the results are unsatisfactory, the cycle is repeated with a revised plan to address the identified issues.

How Are Kaizen and PDCA Related?

The PDCA cycle, its integration with Kaizen principles, the tools and practices used at each stage, and the broader philosophical underpinnings of Kaizen. This level of detail provides a solid foundation for understanding how the PDCA cycle enables the practical implementation of continuous improvement through Kaizen.

1. **Structured approach to improvement:** Kaizen is about making small, incremental changes to improve processes and eliminate waste. The PDCA cycle provides a structured and systematic approach to implementing these improvements. It helps organisations plan, test,

evaluate and standardise improvements in a controlled and organised manner.

2. **Continuous feedback loop:** The cyclical nature of the PDCA cycle aligns perfectly with the Kaizen principle of continuous improvement. By repeating the cycle, organisations can continuously identify new areas for improvement, implement changes, and evaluate their effectiveness, fostering a culture of ongoing progress and refinement.

3. **Employee involvement:** Kaizen heavily emphasises employee involvement and empowerment. The PDCA cycle encourages participation from employees at various stages, such as gathering data, suggesting improvements, and evaluating results. This engagement helps to develop a sense of ownership and commitment to the improvement process.

4. **Data-driven decision-making:** The Check stage of the PDCA cycle emphasises the importance of collecting and analysing data to evaluate the effectiveness of implemented changes. This data-driven approach is crucial in Kaizen, as it helps organisations make informed decisions based on evidence rather than assumptions.

5. **Standardisation and knowledge sharing:** The Act stage of the PDCA cycle ensures that successful improvements are standardised and incorporated into the regular process. This standardisation facilitates

knowledge sharing and enables the organisation to build upon previous improvements, which is a key principle of Kaizen.

PCDA in a Nutshell

1. The fundamental essence of Kaizen is repeating the PDCA cycle continuously. This cyclical process is crucial for driving ongoing improvement.
2. The breakdown of each stage (Plan, Do, Check, Act) and the specific tools/practices used in each stage provide practical guidance on operationalising the PDCA cycle.
3. The transition from a successful PDCA cycle to the SDCA (Standardise, Do, Check, Act) cycle for maintenance and sustaining improvements is an important point.
4. Explaining the importance of standardisation and its benefits within the context of Kaizen reinforces why it is a critical component of the improvement process.
5. Your perspective on Kaizen as a philosophy that challenges the status quo, involves everyone, and requires a mindset shift towards continuous improvement aligns with the fundamental principles of this approach.

17

Conquering Fear and Stress

Fear of change is an intrinsic part of human experience, often arising in response to even minor changes. This fear is rooted in the brain's physiological responses—when fear takes hold, it can hinder creativity, adaptability and success. The incremental approach of Kaizen offers a stealthy solution to this innate quality of the human brain. Instead of requiring extensive counselling to understand and overcome the fear of change, Kaizen allows individuals to sidestep these fears through small, achievable steps.

By setting easily achievable goals, such as organising a single paper clip on a cluttered desk, Kaizen enables people to make progress without triggering the alarm bells in the brain's amygdala. This gradual, unassuming approach allows individuals to navigate change and improvement without the debilitating effects of fear taking hold. Kaizen's focus on small, iterative steps helps bypass the brain's natural resistance to change, empowering people to achieve their goals and embrace progress in a less threatening way.

Kaizen's stepwise methodology provides a practical, brain-friendly solution to the universal human challenge of overcoming the fear of change while simultaneously unlocking creativity, adaptability and success. Kaizen's small, incremental steps can lead to profound changes by rewiring the brain's neural pathways.

As the small, Kaizen-inspired steps continue, the brain's cortex becomes more actively engaged. This kickstarts the process of the brain creating new 'software'— forming new neural pathways and building up habits aligned with the desired change. Over time, as this mental 'software' becomes more established, the initial resistance to change begins to weaken. What was once daunting or intimidating gradually becomes more natural and comfortable. The person may even find themselves exceeding their own expectations, as the new neural networks and habits take hold.

This illustrates the powerful neurological mechanisms at play when Kaizen's approach is applied. The gradual, non-threatening nature of the small steps allows the brain to adapt and rewire itself, ultimately making the desired change feel effortless and intrinsically motivated, rather than forced or resisted. It's a remarkable example of how Kaizen can leverage the brain's own neural plasticity to overcome the fear of change.

Fight-or-Flight

Kaizen's approach of taking small, actionable steps is effective in overcoming the fear of change by addressing the brain's natural 'fight-or-flight' response. When faced with the prospect of change or a challenging creative task, the brain can often trigger a fear response, priming the body for either fleeing the situation or confronting it directly. However, these instinctual reactions are not always the most productive options, especially when it comes to achieving long-term goals.

Kaizen's focus on small, manageable steps provides an alternative outlet for the brain's need to 'do something' in the face of fear or creative blockage. Instead of resorting to avoidance behaviours like running away from challenges or watching TV, the Kaizen practitioner can appease the brain's distress by taking a small, non-threatening action—like simply writing down three musical notes.

As the brain's alarms gradually subside, this small act of progress helps reawaken access to the brain's higher cortical functions. The creative juices start flowing again, allowing the person to gradually build momentum without becoming overwhelmed by the fear of the bigger, more daunting task.

By providing these easily achievable 'safety valves', Kaizen helps bypass the brain's instinctual fight-or-flight response, allowing the individual to stay engaged and make meaningful progress, even in the face of change or creative challenges. It's a powerful way to outsmart the brain's innate resistance and unlock its full potential.

Rewiring the Brain's Response to Change

The human brain is inherently programmed to resist change, as a protective mechanism against perceived threats. However, Kaizen's approach of taking small, incremental steps can effectively rewire the nervous system to overcome this natural resistance. By starting with tiny, manageable actions, Kaizen is able to accomplish several key objectives:

1. **'Unstick' the brain from creative blocks or mental inertia:** The small steps provide a gentle nudge that gets the brain re-engaged and activated, overcoming the paralysis of fear or uncertainty.
2. **Bypass the brain's fight-or-flight response:** Rather than triggering the panic and avoidance associated with major changes, the small steps are non-threatening enough to avoid setting off those alarm bells.
3. **Create new neural connections and pathways**: With each small win, the brain begins to build new associations and habits, forming an enthusiastic neural 'software' that supports the desired change.

As this new 'software' takes hold, the brain starts to actively participate in and drive the change process forward. What were once daunting, overwhelming goals become achievable and even exciting, as the brain's plasticity allows it to rapidly progress towards the target.

In this way, Kaizen's deceptively simple steps snowball into truly transformative leaps, as the brain rewires itself to embrace and even crave the change. It's a powerful demonstration of how the mind can be gently and strategically reprogrammed to overcome its own innate resistance.

Stress . . . or Fear?

In today's medical context, the sensation triggered by a new challenge or significant goal is often termed as stress, yet for generations, it was simply known as fear. Interestingly, successful individuals tend to confront fear directly rather than using clinical terms like anxiety or stress. When adults seek help for emotional distress, they typically use terms such as stress, anxiety, depression, nervousness or tension. Conversely, children are more likely to express their emotions using simpler terms like scared, sad or afraid.

The variance in word choice between children and adults stems more from their expectations rather than the symptoms themselves. Children recognise the inherent lack of control they have over the world around them; they can't dictate their parents' moods or their teachers' behaviour. Therefore, they accept fear as a natural aspect of life. Conversely, adults often believe they should be able to exert control over their circumstances. When fear arises, it feels incongruent with this belief, leading them to categorise it as a psychiatric issue like stress or anxiety. Fear is thus viewed as a disorder to be neatly labelled and contained.

This perspective on fear can be counterproductive. Believing that life should always be orderly sets one up for panic and disappointment. Expecting things like new jobs, relationships, or health goals to be effortless can lead to frustration and bewilderment when fear inevitably surfaces. In such cases, individuals may resort to extreme and unconscious measures to banish fear without even realising it.

During challenging and frightening times, we often seek solutions in familiar or comfortable places rather than confronting the uncomfortable truths that hold real solutions. For instance, someone afraid of intimacy might prioritise changing jobs or relocating to a new city to advance their career rather than facing their fear of closeness. Similarly, individuals neglecting their health or are unhappy in their marriage might divert themselves by investing in a new home instead. Those struggling with self-esteem might resort to drastic measures like cosmetic surgery or crash diets, focusing on external changes rather than addressing their inner struggles. It's essential not to succumb to these common barriers to change, which can induce guilt or frustration, leading to abandonment of efforts to improve oneself.

Conflict is an inherent aspect of being human; if controlling our actions were effortless, society would likely be much more peaceful, and headlines vastly different. Instead of viewing difficult times as negative, we can perceive fear as a valuable signal from our bodies, indicating a challenge ahead. The intensity of our emotions, including fear, often correlates with the importance of our goals and aspirations. By reframing fear in this context, we can mitigate its distressing effects. During trying times, acknowledging fear as a natural response, rather than a hindrance, can help us maintain hope and optimism. This mindset encourages us to take small steps forward despite fear's presence, gradually loosening its grip.

Rather than berating ourselves for consistent tardiness or resigning to the belief that punctuality is beyond our capabilities, we can approach the situation with kindness and understanding. By acknowledging the fear underlying our behaviour, we can take gentle, incremental steps to address it. For example, simply envisioning a positive interaction with a challenging coworker can be a small yet meaningful step forward. Over time, these small actions can rewire our habits and thought patterns. In the following chapters, I'll delve into the specifics of Kaizen, a philosophy centred around making continuous, small improvements. Through these methods, we can confront and even transform our relationship with fear.

Even positive changes can evoke fear. Attempts to achieve goals through drastic or revolutionary methods often backfire because they amplify fear. However, the incremental steps of Kaizen have a calming effect on the brain's fear response, promoting rational thinking and fostering creativity. By taking small, manageable steps, we can gradually overcome fear and pave the way for lasting progress. Kaizen can be a highly effective approach for combating stress and the fear of change within an organisation.

Addressing Stress Through Kaizen

Kaizen's focus on continuous improvement and incremental changes helps alleviate the overwhelming nature of large-scale transformations. By breaking down problems into smaller, manageable steps, Kaizen reduces the pressure and anxiety that often accompanies significant changes. Employees feel empowered to tackle issues one step at a time, fostering a sense of control and agency. The collaborative nature of Kaizen also encourages teamwork and shared problem-solving, which can provide much-needed support and camaraderie during stressful periods. Furthermore, the Kaizen mindset emphasises celebrating small wins, which boosts morale and helps employees stay motivated, even in the face of challenging circumstances.

Overcoming the Fear of Change

Kaizen inherently addresses the fear of change by normalising it as a constant and expected part of the improvement process. Rather than viewing change as a threat, Kaizen teaches employees to embrace it as an opportunity. The Kaizen approach focuses on gradual, incremental changes, which are less disruptive and easier to adapt to compared to sudden, sweeping transformations. By involving employees in the Kaizen process and empowering them to identify and implement improvements, the fear of change is reduced. Employees become active participants in the change, rather than passive recipients. Additionally, the transparent communication and collaborative nature of Kaizen help alleviate the uncertainty and anxiety that often accompanies organisational changes.

By cultivating a Kaizen mindset and embedding its principles throughout the organisation, leaders can create an environment that is more resilient to stress and adaptive to change. Employees feel supported, engaged and empowered to navigate the inevitable transformations that come with continuous improvement, ultimately leading to a more agile and successful organisation.

❑

Don't Be Hard on Yourself

When applying Kaizen to reshape your inner voice and transform habitual patterns, it's crucial not to be harsh or judgemental with yourself along the way. Beating yourself up for stumbling or not immediately reaching your goals goes completely against the mindset required for sustainable self-improvement.

During challenging periods, the absolute worst thing you can do is layer intense self-criticism on top of it all. This will only amplify your struggles and make you feel exponentially worse. When you inevitably experience setbacks or lapses in your Kaizen process, meet them with understanding and kindness rather than anger at yourself.

The Kaizen approach is about making small, persistent, incremental adjustments—not drastic, punishing overhauls. If you find yourself falling back into negative self-talk or old counterproductive patterns, that's okay. Don't judge or berate yourself. Simply acknowledge it with compassion. Remind yourself that this is all part of the iterative process of stepwise growth.

Then, when you're feeling a bit more grounded and resilient, you can gently restart your practice of interspersing more positive, nurturing self-talk throughout your day. Rebuild the new habit slowly and patiently through modest, repeated efforts, not harsh self-demands. Consistent small steps will gradually reprogramme the automatic negative voice.

The path of true self-improvement and enduring change comes through having an attitude of encouragement, acceptance and non-judgement towards yourself, especially during life's inevitable rough periods. Met with kindness and patience rather than criticism, any lapses become just temporary detours before returning to the iterative Kaizen practice of incremental self-optimisation.

Difficult Times As a Strict Teacher

Experiencing difficult life challenges such as job loss, the end of a relationship, or the death of a loved one can feel utterly devastating and destabilising. However, they also present opportunities for profound self-discovery and growth in resilience. The Kaizen approach is to find pride in your ability to keep putting one foot in front of the other each day, no matter how incrementally. Continuing to move forward is an achievement in itself.

In the Japanese and Sino written languages, there isn't a single character representing 'crisis'. Instead, the concept is expressed by combining the characters for 'danger' and 'opportunity'. This duality reminds us that even in life's most perilous situations, there exist seeds of positive reinvention if we remain open to them. When you're in the depths of adversity, it can be extremely difficult to see the potential upsides. However, maintaining the Kaizen mindset of making small, persistent adjustments over time allows you to gradually reshape your perspective. Each day, practice reframing just a bit more toward recognising the 'opportunity' alongside the 'danger'.

Reinforce this. Past relationship breakups that initially seemed earth-shattering can eventually lead you to more fulfilling partnerships. Similarly, being made redundant from what once seemed a dream job could turn out to be a catalyst for an even better professional path shortly after. Viewed through the Kaizen lens, those deeply painful experiences became critical inflection points for self-improvement and growth.

The key is understanding that, like any profound transformation, positives rarely emerge suddenly after crises. Instead, the slowly compounding incremental adjustments in how you relate to adversity eventually allow you to evolve from it. Have compassion for the struggle, but keep making those modest thought-pattern shifts. Actively seek out potentialities amid the risks. Let each day's small, encouraging inner voice expand your perspective a bit more.

Over time and with patience, the 'opportunities' come more into focus. By applying the principles of Kaizen way even in the darkest times, you ultimately reinvent yourself into a more resilient, wiser version. The potential for progress and renewal remains ever-present if you nurture it iteratively. Your experience with Kaizen and continuous self-improvement is unlikely to follow a straight, uninterrupted path. We are all initially highly motivated to build new positive habits or discard unhealthy ones. However, it's natural for that motivation to ebb and flow as other priorities and curveballs from life inevitably get in the way.

Major life disruptions can make it tremendously challenging to stay on the Kaizen course. During such stressful periods, it becomes tempting to revert to old, comforting behaviours, even if they are counterproductive. Similarly, any dramatic changes to your daily environment like moving, changing jobs, retiring or having a baby can spark a craving for the familiarity of routine, even an unhealthy one. It's crucial to understand that Kaizen is a lifelong commitment to iterative growth, not a short burst towards perfection. There will be times when your motivation understandably wavers or you hit periods of significant hardship—unless you're the luckiest person alive. That's okay and to be expected. No one is perfect, and the goal of Kaizen is not to achieve some imagined ideal of permanent perfection.

Rather, Kaizen is about viewing life itself as an exciting journey of endless opportunities for self-refinement and taking a long-term perspective. Even when you falter or life sidetracks your progress, quickly forgive yourself and simply restart your incremental practice of self-optimisation when you gain your footing again. The core of Kaizen is to make persistent adjustments through a mindset of patience and self-compassion. By taking this nurturing, non-judgemental attitude through the inevitable ups and downs, you steadily build powerful, positive habits and steadily improve your relationship with yourself.

Progress may not happen in a linear fashion, but that iterative, step-by-step growth through the winding paths of life's journey is what Kaizen is all about. Each day presents a fresh chance to make another modest step towards your aspirations. Perfection is not required, just a commitment to taking those incremental strides whenever you can.

The Cycle of Punishing

The overly critical self-talk that many people engage in is antithetical to the core ideas behind Kaizen—the philosophy of continuous, incremental improvement. Those who berate themselves with harsh inner voices are essentially working against their own progress and personal growth. True self-improvement requires nurturing encouragement, not destructive criticism.

The Kaizen mindset is about embracing the journey of ongoing optimisation. There is no process so perfect that it cannot be improved through minor tweaks and refinements over time. Similarly, developing a more encouraging inner dialogue requires patience and the accumulation of small changes—consciously catching negative thoughts and reframing them with kinder self-talk.

Ultimately, life's most successful people don't browbeat themselves into achievement. Instead, they engage in a Kaizen-like practice of gently, firmly coaching themselves forward through an asset-based lens, focused on their efforts, abilities and potential. It's about making incremental strides to improve their inner processes for relating to themselves. Each time a negative thought arises, they view it as an opportunity to Kaizen—to optimise their mindset through a small, course-correcting adjustment towards more nurturing self-belief. Consistent application of Kaizen in this manner compounds over time into substantially more productive and positive inner dialogue.

The overly critical inner voice that many of us often struggle with is essentially outdated programming that was installed in the midbrain at an early development—maybe echoes of harsh interactions with parents, teachers or coping mechanisms formed before we knew better ways of self-relating. Regardless of its origins, this negative self-talk has become an automatic, habitual response.

To transform this into a more nurturing inner voice, we must engage the cerebral cortex—the thinking brain capable of constructive coaching rather than primal rebuking. Fortunately, the cortex is highly malleable and can reshape habits through repetition, much like how advertisers use repeated messaging to create new consumer behaviours.

Through a Kaizen process of incremental practices, we can gradually reprogramme the inner voice. Multiple times per day, catch yourself engaging in negative self-talk. Pause, and visualise someone you deeply admire performing that same task or facing the same situation. Imagine the supportive words of encouragement and compassionate tone you would use with them. Then, turn that same affirming self-talk inward and repeat it to yourself out loud. The process isn't about eliminating the critical voice entirely through a dramatic overhaul. Such an aggressive approach isn't sustainable. Instead, it's a Kaizen of patiently counter-programming through gentle, incremental repetitions of more positive thoughts.

The cortex is predisposed to reshaping habits through repeated exposure. By making small, regular deposits of nurturing self-talk into your cognitive framework, you incrementally build new neural pathways. Over time, these new mental patterns compound until perspective and affirmative self-coaching become automated and habitual.

Once the foundation of more encouraging inner dialogue is firmly laid through this Kaizen process, you can then build upon it through continued optimisations. Apply this asset-based, compassionate mindset as you Kaizen towards your larger goals through iterative refinements. Achieved through modest, persistent steps, profound personal transformations emerge.

The Kaizen Path to Overcoming Isolation

The importance of community, support networks, and asking for help when needed aligns perfectly with the principles of Kaizen.

The myth of rugged self-reliance is just that—a myth. Even the most outwardly successful people rely on networks of support to help them through challenging times. Isolating yourself or your team behind walls when facing difficulties sets you up for depression, despair, and deprivation of valuable outside resources.

While taking small, incremental Kaizen steps can provide some forward momentum, they become exponentially more effective when allowing those steps to guide you towards people who can offer concrete assistance or emotional support to ease your fears and re-energise your productivity. However, asking for help doesn't come naturally to many people; it requires developing new habits and mindset. You can train yourself to become more comfortable reaching out for help through Kaizen practices like the following:

Twice daily, ask yourself: "Who could I ask for help?" and "What kind of help could I request?" At first, you may draw a blank. But by consistently reflecting on those questions, potential answers will start bubbling up.

The story of the couple who owned a small business illustrates this well. When the wife fell ill, they struggled until they made a Kaizen practice of regularly vocalising "Who/what can we ask for help with?" Initially, they had no ideas, but within days, they began considering untapped resources like professional networks, family, hospitals and financial assistance programmes.

This simple act of reframing their perspective towards "What aid is available?" instead of "We're on our own" opened up new solution pathways. It provided relief just realising they didn't have to face their challenges alone. Applying Kaizen to build the habit of actively looking for potential supportive people/groups to aid you makes asking for help feel far less daunting. You expand your perspective through small, persistent steps until that abundance mindset becomes second nature.

Instead of unproductive isolation, Kaizen encourages an iterative process of first identifying and then taking modest actions to engage your personal and professional communities for assistance and encouragement. This fosters an empowering positive spiral where consistent small efforts create increasing resilience and connectivity.

Mind Scripture: Asking for Help

Visualisation and practicing 'mind sculpting' are valuable techniques for building comfort and confidence in asking for help. Integrating this practice is a fantastic way to apply Kaizen principles to this often difficult but important skill.

The Kaizen technique of mind sculpture—vividly imagining a challenging scenario by engaging all your senses—can be extremely helpful for getting more comfortable with reaching out for assistance when needed. By doing mental rehearsals in small, incremental steps, you gradually reshape your mindset until the previously daunting task feels manageable.

Practice Mind Sculpting

1. Close your eyes and visualise the person you want to ask for help standing before you. Imagine every vivid detail—their appearance, the surroundings, and immerse yourself in any sounds/smells associated with the scene.
2. Now visualise yourself calmly and clearly requesting for assistance. Notice your posture, tone of voice, and the specific words you use.
3. Then imagine their potential responses—how will you feel/react if they say no or yes?
4. If this exercise feels difficult at first, start with just 3-5 seconds of visualisation per day. Slowly increase the duration in small increments as it becomes easier.
5. Also increase the frequency from once to twice per day as you build the new mental pathway.

The couple who owned the small business struggled to actually ask for help, even after identifying potential sources of support. Using the mind sculpting technique allowed them to simulate the experience of making requests in low-risk incremental steps.

Within just a few days of these brief daily visualisations, they felt ready to start actually reaching out to others. To their relief, they found their community had been hoping for opportunities to lend assistance.

By using mind sculpture as a Kaizen tool—gently and persistently refining the same mental skill through small, incremental steps—you can overcome hesitancy around asking for help. You reprogramme your instinctive discomfort into courage and confidence through visualisation repetitions. The small, compounding efforts reshape your mindset. This allows you to eventually take the vital real-world action of seeking support from your networks, secure in the knowledge that you've thoroughly prepared yourself mentally. Consistent Kaizen practice forges resilient new response pathways until reaching out feels natural.

Streetlight Searching

"The man under the streetlight was looking for the brightest spot.

He'd been looking so intently that he 'forgot' what he was actually searching for."

This brings up an excellent point about the importance of clearly defining your goals and desired outcomes when applying Kaizen principles. Without clarity on where you're ultimately trying to direct your incremental efforts, it's easy to get caught up in 'streetlighting'— looking for solutions in the wrong places.

Start small by checking in with yourself once or twice a day. Simply ask "What is my goal here?" or "What am I truly hoping to achieve?" Don't judge whatever initial answers surface, just observe them mindfully. Over time, your repetitive self-inquiry will bring your driving objectives into sharper focus.

Incorporate mindfulness into your routine by regularly pausing to notice when you feel a sense of satisfaction, fulfilment or resonance with an activity or pursuit. These are clues pointing you towards your intrinsic values and sources of meaning that shape your deeper goals.

Engage in short, free-form writing sessions where you riff stream-of-consciousness style about what really matters to you and what you want out of your career, relationships, finances, etc. Engage in this brain dump regularly without censoring. Over time, patterns and themes will emerge, revealing core goals.

When you catch yourself feeling stressed or frustrated, pause to reflect on the particular goal or expectation that is causing that negativity. Identify and separate whether it is a misalignment with an external demand versus one of your own primary objectives.

Share what's on your mind with trusted friends, family or colleagues and solicit their perspectives. Sometimes an outside view can shine light on goals or motivations we have trouble seeing in ourselves. The key is to use iterative, low-pressure techniques to gradually bring your goals into focus through small, frequent check-ins. Be patient and avoid judging yourself. Clarity will compound through the Kaizen process until your vision for what you truly want becomes crystal clear. With that long-term aim defined, you can then align all your incremental Kaizen steps towards making progress.

Steps Towards Integration

- **Step 1:** Make a detailed list describing what a fully successful life looks like for you personally. If this comes easily, you likely don't have issues with a lack of clarity. But if the process feels difficult and your answers are vague, move to the next step.
- **Step 2:** Each morning, adopt a gentle approach and ask yourself, "What do I want from my personal life, career, and health?" Without being judgemental, allow your thoughts to arise and welcome all responses.
- **Step 3:** Over the course of weeks or months, compile all the gathered insights into a cohesive list.
- **Step 4:** Once you have the list, use a Kaizen visualisation practice in your routine. Spend just 2-3 seconds per day vividly imagining yourself having achieved all those listed goals and aspirations. Gradually increase the duration by a few seconds each week, adding an extra daily session as you progress.
- **Step 5:** As you build this habit of visualisation through small incremental steps, you may spontaneously find

yourself taking modest real-world actions towards actualising one of those goals without even trying.

The beauty of this process is how it gradually cultivates clarity in a gentle, reassuring way through small, bite-sized efforts. You aren't forcefully trying to decide your purposes all at once.

Instead, you nurture them into consciousness over time through Kaizen practices like:

- Morning check-ins
- Compiling an aspirational list incrementally
- Visualisation repetitions that are extended patiently

These deceptively modest activities create subtle but compounding shifts, allowing your goals to come into focus organically. The visualisation acts as a form of mental practice and reinforcement.

Before long, you've honed an inspiring vision for your ideal life in a low-pressure way. That laser-focused clarity then naturally guides you toward taking real-world Kaizen steps to start actualising those aims. This iterative process aligns perfectly with core Kaizen principles of making small, persistent adjustments over time to achieve profound transformations. You've optimised your goal-setting through patience and self-compassion.